NEVER AGAIN

MATTHEW TELLES

For my family

CONTENTS

Never Again

CHAPTER 1

Katie

"Katie," I heard my mum yell from downstairs, "It's time to get up. You don't want to be late for school!"

"I'll be down in a minute!" I shouted back, sleepily. Checking my alarm, it read Seven o'clock in the morning.

Shit!

I was going to be late.

I got up and started rushing around; having a shower, brushing my teeth, and then getting dressed.

When I finally got downstairs my breakfast was already on the table. Pancakes and bacon. One of my favourite meals. As I devoured my food, I thanked my mom through a mouthful.

"You're welcome sweetie," she replied, smiling.

My mum had always been one of my best friends. I had other friends and some had been there for me like my mom had, but she was my role model, the person I aspired to be. Through everything, I tried to do the same thing for her, even though she said it wasn't necessary.

"Thank you, honey, but it's enough just having you here." She always said.

I could tell how much she appreciated it though.

I finished my food and then got up to hug her.

"Thanks for the food mum," I said, "It was really nice."

"You're welcome. Now don't forget to take all your books." She said, with one eyebrow raised. "And don't go on your phone during class otherwise I'll have to take it away."

I sheepishly smiled, scratching the back of my neck, and replied. "Yes, mum."

We heard a car horn outside. That must be Jessica.

"Enjoy your first day back!"

"Bye mum!" I shouted as I ran out the door.

I ran outside and saw Jessica's car was parked in front of me.

Jessica loved her cute little ruby red Honda S2000. It was her prized possession and she even gave it the name James. She said that she called it James because that is the name of her spirit animal. The girl was so weird.

Jessica and I had been friends for 10 years. She was a tall blonde who usually wore her hair up, accentuating her slim face. We went to the same school when we were younger and she once knocked me over, spilling my food everywhere, but she was nice to me and helped me pick it back up; even offering to share hers with me.

"Hey Kate," Jessica said, "Long time no see."

"It's been three days," I replied with a small chuckle.

"I know, but it feels like a long time." She said with a pout, slapping me lightly on the shoulder.

We talked on the way to school; her complaining about her mum, and how strict she had been lately and me mostly listening.

"She's even getting me to do extra homework," Jessica muttered, grimacing. "All because I got a C."

"It can't be that bad. I'm sure your mum only wants to help," I mentioned, trying not to laugh at her face.

2

"Yeah," Jessica groaned, "I'm sure she does. But that doesn't mean it's fun."

We arrived at school fifteen minutes later and saw our other friends waiting for us at the entrance.

We both met Jill and Hugh two years ago.

Jill was an energetic person, always moving around or talking. She didn't see it, but she was beautiful and had a ton of guys drooling over her. With her perfect hair and shiny brunette curls rolling down her back she was a bombshell. While her personality annoyed some people, I didn't mind because I struggled to start conversations with people, so it was nice to have a friend like her around. Especially considering how her personality seemed to rub off on the people around her.

Hugh, on the other hand, was the clown of the group. Always goofing around and making us all laugh. He was quiet but he'd swoop in at the perfect time, making us giggle. Although Hugh seemed like he was not a serious person, if you needed him, he would be there for you. Hugh loved playing football and thus, was mildly popular, especially with the ladies, with his black ear-length hair and chestnut eyes. He also worked out every day to keep in top shape.

"Hey Kate!" Jill said as she walked over to us, "Good to see you sober."

I blushed thinking about the last time we had seen each other.

We had all got completely wasted - me more than anyone else and as a result, I ended up making a complete fool of myself by throwing up all over Jill's new top and in the Uber we took home. It's something they'd teased me about ever since.

"Hi guys, it's good to see you again," I said while hugging them both, a big smile on my face as it felt like a long time since I had seen them.

"It's good to see you too," Hugh said, with a big grin on his face. "It feels like years since we last saw you."

"Oh, stop it," Jessica said, rolling her eyes. "It's only been a week since we've all seen each other."

"Come on guys, stop arguing or we'll be late," Jill responded while lightly laughing, skipping away from us to her class. That girl.

We split up and went to our separate classes. Unfortunately, we didn't have the same schedules, although it would've been pretty lucky if we did. We ended up only having a few classes with each other.

Just as the teacher was about to start the lesson, the door swung right open and in walked Blake.

Blake was the 'bad boy' of the school. Really tough. All he did was get into detention and sleep around. It was not cool. If anything, it made me want to know less about him.

"What is the meaning of this, Mr. Hardridge," My English teacher, Mrs. Thornton, said. "Being late and then interrupting my class?!"

"Sorry," He said with a grin, slightly slouching. "I had things to do."

I heard some noises at the back of the room and turned to see what it was. It was a few girls staring dreamily at him. I couldn't help but sigh.

I had to admit that he was a good-looking guy. Blonde hair, blue eyes, with the body of a god. That was all the girls saw. They didn't see how they were just getting played and that it was their own fault. Blake was bad news and I was just thankful I hadn't encountered him over the summer.

"That will not be tolerated in my class. I suggest you start appearing on time, otherwise I'll have to give you detention." She advised sternly.

The smirk stayed on his face as he eyed the room in search of a desk. His eyes found mine and I quickly looked away, but not quickly enough as he walked over to me and sat right next to me.

Class started and I focused on the teacher. The lesson was almost over when I felt something hit me from one side, only to look over and see Blake's cocky face staring back at me.

"Hey," he said, "My name is Blake."

"I know who you are," I answered in a sarcastic tone looking away from him, "Please, I'm trying to focus on the lesson, so we can talk later."

I looked at him out of the corner of my eye only to find him staring at me with one eyebrow raised. I quickly turned away, focusing on the lesson.

"Fine by me. I'm looking forward to it." He said, with a low chuckle.

I ignored him for the rest of the lesson and didn't see him for the rest of the day. Instead of dwelling on it, I hung out with my friends during lunch and with Jessica during math. The only lesson I have with her.

"I'll see you guys tomorrow." I said.

Hugh and Jill gave me a hug and went off to their homes while Jessica drove us back to my house. We always hung out after school. We arrived at my house a few minutes later to find the house empty.

Mum would still be at work for a few more hours.

"So, what do you want to do first," Jessica asked, "Homework, or watch a movie?"

"Definitely homework, then we'll have as much time as we want to do whatever after," I said, grabbing my school bag and shuffling upstairs.

"Sounds good," Jessica replied, "Let's get to work then."

I was so glad that it was finally the weekend. Jill, Hugh, Jessica, and I had plans for today; we were going to a beach party.

I couldn't decide what to wear, so I called Jessica to help me find something nice. We ended up finding something quickly and so decided to spend the rest of our time hanging out watching The Flash.

"I can't believe Barry is actually going to go to prison," Jessica exclaimed, "Do you think he'll be there for the rest of the season?"

"Of course not," I scoffed, "It is called 'The Flash' so they have to have him in it."

"You're right, I don't know what I was thinking," The said, slapping her forehead.

"Well, anyways, it's time to go now, otherwise, we'll be late," I said, pulling Jessica up, "Let's go."

We arrived at the party, having picked up Jill and Hugh along the way.

"Wow!" I exclaimed, "There are so many people here!"

There were at least two hundred people all crowded onto the beach: some from our school and some looking like they were college age. Music boomed from the speakers that were placed a fair distance away from the fire, giving people enough room to dance; or get their eardrums severely damaged.

"This is the biggest party I've been to in a long time," Said Jill, "I only recognise about half of the people here."

My eyes widened as I surveyed the surroundings. Scanning through the sea of people, my eyes landed on someone that I recognised - Blake standing among a group of people. The people with him seemed too superficially friendly, especially one of the girls from school who had her arms clutched around him and was hanging on for dear life. I kind of felt sorry for him until my brain actually registered the feeling of pity as I remembered how much of a douche he could be, and all sympathy left me.

"I'm going to go get us drinks," Said Hugh, "I'll be back in a minute."

"I'll come with you," Jill said, "It'll be quicker."

"Alright, let's go," Hugh replied.

While Hugh and Jill walked off towards the bar Jessica and I talked about what all of us were going to do when they came back. In the end, we decided to just go with the flow for a few hours and then make our way back to our houses.

"Hey, we're back," Hugh said, handing us our drinks. "So, what are we doing?"

"Let's dance first," Jessica said. "Then we'll see."

"Sounds good. Let's go." Jill replied.

We danced for around half an hour before I saw Blake out of the corner of my eye. He was eyeing me, unnerving me.

I turned towards him and frowned. He just smirked back and walked off into the crowd. I shook my head and carried on having a good time.

"So, want to go home yet?" Jessica asked, pulling me to the side.

"I'll get one more drink and then we will go." I said, "You want anything?"

"No thanks," Jessica said, "I'll stay here. Meet me after."

I walked off towards the makeshift bar and ordered a drink. I was walking back sipping my drink when I felt a hand on my shoulder. I whipped around, only to see Blake.

"Hey." His tired voice rumbled.

"What do you want?" I asked tiredly. Although on the inside I was quite annoyed that I had been interrupted.

"I want to know if you want to chill out with me?"

"No, why would I want that?" I said, storming off.

Why was I angry with him?

I must have had one too many drinks because nothing I was doing was making sense anymore. Even to myself.

I would apologise tomorrow.

I walked back to my friends and reminded them that we had to leave. We dropped Hugh off first and then Jill, leaving me as the last one for Jessica to drop off.

"I'll see you tomorrow." Jessica hugged me. "Bye girl!"

"See you tomorrow," I replied, grinning goofily.

I walked into my house and saw my mum sat at the table, waiting up for me.

"Hey mum," I walked over to her, "What are you doing up?"

"Oh, hey honey, I was just waiting up for you."

"You don't have to do that mum," I said, yawning.

"I know I don't, but I want to." She said with a smile.

"Goodnight mum," I reply, giving her a hug.

"Sleep well, sweetie."

I walked upstairs slowly, making sure I didn't fall over as I was tipsy and really tired.

When I reached my room, I unlocked the door and stepped inside. I went through the motions of getting ready for bed; had a shower, and then put on my pyjamas. I of course did not forget to brush my teeth. I went to put my clothes away only to hear the slight noise of paper being scrunched. I felt around in the pocket for a moment before withdrawing my hand which held a piece of paper that read:

I want to get to know you better

- B

Who the hell was 'B'?

I didn't know and right then, I was frankly too tired to figure it out. I finished getting ready and jumped into bed, relaxing and closing my eyes. Quickly falling asleep, I dreamed of a mysterious boy with blue eyes.

I woke up the next morning with a bit of a headache. I was very lucky that it was the weekend and I didn't have to go to school. I didn't think I would have been able to hide my hangover.

Still in bed, I checked my phone while lying down on my back. As I did so, it started ringing, startling me. I dropped my phone on my face and let out a groan as the pain in my head multiplied.

I sat up gingerly and grabbed my phone. Putting it up to my ear, I answered it.

"Hello?" I let out, as a grimace overtook my face.

"Hey Kate," Jessica said cheerily, "I was wondering if you wanted to go shopping with me?"

"Yeah, I will. Just give me about thirty minutes to get ready." I mumbled, rubbing my head and sitting up further.

"Okay, that's fine. See you soon!" Not caring that I was not enthusiastic about her proposition.

"Bye," I replied and hung up.

I got up and had a shower, brushing my teeth after.

Having got dressed I went downstairs. When I got there, I found a note from mum.

I'm going on a business trip for the next few days. I have left fifty pounds on the table, and I fully stocked the fridge before I left. Make sure to call me every night and make sure you're responsible. Love you lots – Mum

Smiling, I put down the note, picked up the money, and stuffed it in my pocket. My head was still hurting so I decided to take some ibuprofen before I left to help make the day a lot more manageable.

We arrived at our local shop and exited the car. Jessica and I always ate before we bought anything so we went into our 'go-to food place' - McDonald's.

"The usual?" Jessica asked with a slight smile.

"Sure," I answered offhandedly, distracted by someone with blonde hair that had their back to me. I felt like I recognised them, but I couldn't place where from.

I was snapped out of my thoughts as Jessica tapped me on the shoulder.

"Here you go." She said, giving me a smile.

"Thanks." I said, glancing back at the boy only for him to be staring back at me smirking.

Blake.

I quickly glanced away and tucked into my food, a blush creeping onto my cheeks.

"What?" Jessica asked, noticing my growing redness.

"Nothing," I mumbled, dragging my eyes away from hers and back to my food, pretending I was fully focused on just eating.

"Fine," Jessica said with a huff, "Don't tell me then."

Jessica had always been very perceptive of my moods and good at picking up on what I was feeling. The reason I didn't tell her the truth was because, frankly, I didn't know what was actually going on with me.

We finished up and got up to leave. I took one last look towards Blake but he had gone. I felt a strange twinge of disappointment. I scoffed and shook it off before following Jessica for our quick shopping session.

Four hours later.

"Jessica," I whined, "Let's just go."

"Come on Katie, we've only been out for a few hours," She said exasperatedly while searching the T-shirt rack. "We'll go back soon. Go sit down at the front of the shop and I'll come find you when I'm done, okay?"

"Okay..." I grumbled, walking towards the shop front.

I plopped down and started to analyse people.

The redhead and her boyfriend laughing and joking, having a wonderful time, enjoying each other's company just talking but I noticed the subtle looks they would give each other, or the constant touching, even if it was only for a second.

The brown-haired guy, talking with his friends while walking along towards the game shop enthusiastically conversing about the new game that seemed to have taken the market by storm, Apex Legends? I had been constantly hearing about it but never bothered to check what all the fuss was about.

Then I saw Blake. He was sitting alone watching people like me, his blue eyes searching for someone or something. His gaze seemed heavy and his eyes looked tired.

I was surprised when they snapped onto me. I quickly looked away, embarrassed at being caught looking at him. As I did so, I felt a weird feeling in my gut almost like butterflies?

No, that couldn't be the case. I was probably just hungry.

I gave him a small smile and surprisingly, he smiled back at me.

I was thinking of going over to him to apologise for yesterday when Jessica came out of the store.

"Ready to go?" She said, waiting for me to respond, with a smile on her face.

"Definitely," I said, cheerfully bouncing up and walking with her.

She started talking to me about what she had bought but I wasn't paying attention. I was looking back at Blake who was staring at me with an intense gaze, whilst having a neutral expression on his face. I couldn't pry my eyes away from him. Something about him was drawing me in.

I must just want to get to know him a bit more, that is all, I thought. Quickly, I dismissed this thought as ludicrous.

"-so then..." I heard Jessica trail off. "Are you even listening to me?"

"Sorry," I said, with a sheepish smile, "What were you saying?"

She looked at me with a critical eye before carrying on with what she had been saying. I glanced back at where he was, but he was no longer there. I distracted myself by focusing on the conversation with Jessica. Although, even with that I wasn't able to get Blake out of my mind.

Sunday.

The last day of the weekend before I had to head to school again.

I couldn't go out with anyone today as I knew I had to work hard in school, or I wouldn't be able to go where I wanted.

I knew Jill and High wanted to go travelling around the world for a year or two before going to university and so they lived their lives by taking risks and having a lot of fun. But the thought of travelling around the world for that length of time, even with a friend to go along with, was scary, so I had never even considered it. Especially since I was so adamant about going to university.

Jessica was extremely focused on school, like me, even if it didn't seem like it at times. She just didn't have to study as much because of her great memory, which allowed her to do more during the day around the things that she enjoyed - like shopping.

As opposed to me who struggled to remember my own name some of the time. Stupid, I know.

I hadn't put too much thought on what I wanted to do with myself when I grew up past going to a university, but I definitely knew I wanted to go to one of the top ones in the country, which is why I put so much emphasis on studying, even if I was already up to date in all my classes. I wanted to be ahead of everyone and be ready for university as I knew that learning to work in your own time was a massively underappreciated skill that a lot of people didn't take time to learn.

I never really found any subject extremely hard. In fact, I found quite a few pretty easy and had already started looking into advanced courses online.

A Sunday without any friends or mum around to hang out with usually consisted of studying and watching TV. Today, the show I was into was called 'You' and I definitely understood why it was so popular. Great acting, writing and camera work.

Throughout the day I was constantly getting distracted by the note I received.

Who put it there? How did it get there and why did they do it?

These were all questions I was mulling over as I finally finished all the studying I had planned for that day.

I quickly got bored and decided to walk to the library just to look around and see if they had any new books that I would like to read.

I got ready and then put my shoes on before stepping outside to begin the walk.

Once I arrived, I decided to walk to the fiction section, but it had been moved since I had last come in.

I couldn't be bothered to look around, so I decided to ask one of the employees where it was.

Walking up to a girl that kind of looked familiar, I quickly dismissing that thought and smiling her.

"Excuse me, can you tell me where the fiction section is please?" I said.

The young raven-haired woman turned and smiled at me as she answered, "Sure, follow me."

Following her, we went up the stairs to the second floor and stopped at the back where there was a small sign which mentioned that this was indeed the fiction section.

I thanked her and as she walked away I racked my brain for possibilities as to why she seemed quite familiar to me, but ultimately, I could come up with nothing and decided to get the newest book in the 'BodyGuard' series as I had read all the previous ones and was interested in what this one had to offer.

Taking the book off the shelf, I walked down the stairs to the counter to find the same girl manning this counter too. This time I decided to get curiosity off of my mind and asked her if I knew her.

"Sorry to impose, but I feel like I know you from somewhere?"

"You might have seen me at school as I only graduated last year," she said. Looking me over, she reconsidered. "Or you might have heard of my brother."

"Who is your brother?" I enquired, very interested in the answer.

"Blake Hardridge is my brother," She said, smiling wryly at my shocked face before handing me my book, "Enjoy. I've heard this one is good."

I walked back home still semi surprised that Blake has a sister, and that she seemed like the complete opposite of him. Not just in terms of personality but also life-style.

When I got back home it was dinner time but I didn't have enough food in the house so I just ordered a take away.

As I was eating, I decided to text Jessica to ask if she wanted to stay over. Her reaction was an enthusiastic "sure" before she hung up on me so she could leave.

Around half an hour later she arrived with three bags of snacks.

"You brought all of those for tonight?" I asked, gesturing at the bags she was carrying.

She gave me a look and said, "You know we can eat the whole lot tonight. Don't play with me."

I laughed and agreed, picking up one of the chocolate bars and stuffing it in my mouth.

I woke up later, the TV still on but the volume turned down. It was quiet. Too quiet.

I slowly got up and gingerly made my way over to the door which was ajar.

My heart sped up as I shut it with caution. I cautiously tiptoed back to the couch to check if Jessica was still sleeping or if it had been her that had opened the door.

Unfortunately, she was still on the couch fast asleep, with her head lolled to the side, in what looked like an uncomfortable position.

Deciding to check the rest of the house to make sure nothing else was awry, I set out on that mission.

Silently, I crept around the house, checking that all the windows were locked and shut and that none of the other doors were open that shouldn't have been.

I was starting to calm down when the sound of a floorboard creaking behind me and my fear sky rocketed once more. My heart stopped before I turned around to see a tired-looking Jessica.

"Jesus Christ," I said, releasing the breath I hadn't realised I had been holding. "You scared the fuck out of me."

"Sorry," She mumbled sleepily, "I thought you had come up to go to bed in your room."

Jessica walked past me as I sighed in relief.

Realising I had left my phone downstairs, I went to get it. On the way, I looked out the back-door window and saw shoe prints. A little bit of mud was tracked into the house too

I suddenly felt a sense of dread wash over me as I realised someone had been in the house.

I searched the house for anything that I could see missing but found nothing. The only sign there was, was some household objects having not been where I had put them the night before.

When mum got back, I told her straight that someone had been in and out of the house without any of us seeing them.

She asked me if I was positive and I explained all the discrepancies I had found around the house and the mud tracked in, which hadn't been there when me and Jessica had fallen asleep - I had wiped away the evidence because of my nerves.

She called the police and while they were on their way, I told her how the rest of the night panned out and most of the details I could remember. I was still too shaken up to have fully recalled everything that had transpired.

"What time would you say you first noticed there was someone else in the house?"

One policeman had been questioning me while another two checked for forced entry or any indication that someone had been here.

"At around two in the morning." I answered, suddenly glad that we had a clock stationed in the kitchen.

"And did you see anything unusual or hear anything?" He asked me.

"I heard some noise coming from upstairs," I mentioned, as a shivers climbed up my spine from the mere memory of the previous night. "But by the time I got there, whoever it was had already left the house."

I zoned out as I heard the policeman describe what was going to happen and to call if anything else like this happened again.

After they were all gone, I talked to my mum about the incident as she wanted to know more, although I did know that it was just because she wanted reassurance that I was fine, and I was happy to give that to her.

Later on, after I had spewed all the details of the past night, over and over again, I went up to my room ready to fall fast asleep as the adrenaline had now worn off.

Still feeling a little bit apprehensive I decided to check every corner and crevice to make sure no one had put something in there - someone even.

Firstly, I took my drawers out. One by one. And searched them thoroughly and at a methodically slow pace just to make sure I didn't miss anything.

Next was my wardrobe which was full of my dressier clothes. I didn't wea them a lot anymore but looking through the pile I wished I once again had the confidence to. Those feeling quickly faded as the fear crept back in, but luckily, I also didn't find anything of substance in there, except one of my favourite black tops which I had been looking for, for ages!

I had a couple of boxes in my room for extra storage and so still needed to check them.

The first box was stored at the bottom of my wardrobe and was a bit of a pain to get out as the wardrobe had a lip at the bottom to stop stuff easily falling out and whatever I had put in this box felt like it weighed a ton.

Putting it down on my bed, I opened it and started to make my way through the box, taking out each item and making sure it was mine and not broken. This was a slow process as I had quite a lot of little toys in here that I had kept for no other reason than sentimentality.

Finding nothing, I sighed and painstakingly put everything back into the box, closed it, hefted it into my arms and then shuffled across the floor to put it back. I got to my wardrobe and put it down quite heavily. So heavily in fact that it sounded like the floor had broken.

"Are you okay?!" I heard mum shout from downstairs.

"I'm fine mum," I shouted back, quickly putting things away as I didn't want mum to notice how much this was affecting me. "Just dropped a box."

Once I had confirmed that she wasn't coming up anytime soon I checked the one box to left. Pulling it out from under my bed but left it on the floor. This one didn't have as much in it, so it didn't take anywhere near as long as the other box.

Nothing unusual was in my room.

I felt a massive sense of relief as I put the lid on and pushed it back under my bed. No one had entered my room. Although the rest of the house still felt unsafe, at least I knew that no one had violated my personal privacy.

I flopped down onto my bed, closing my eyes, as I felt the effects of the night before wash over me and I instantly fell sleep.

I woke up six hours later to the smell of freshly cooked food. My stomach rumbled and it made me think of the last time I eaten, which was yesterday.

Rubbing the sleep from my eyes, I got up and headed downstairs slowly as I was still half asleep.

"Hey mum."

"Hello Katie," Mum said with a smile, "I was just about to call you down for dinner."

"I just realised I haven't eaten all day and I'm starving now."

She frowned, "You've got to remember to eat as you're just damaging your body if you don't."

"I won't forget again."

When the food had finished cooking, I put some of the noodles on my plate and slathered them in beef stir-fry.

I headed upstairs with my food as I knew mum would be downstairs doing work and I didn't want to interrupt her.

As I ate the last bit of my food, I heard mum shut her door and could tell by the squeaking sound of the bed that she was going to sleep.

Quietly moving out of my room, I went and put my plate in the dishwasher but didn't turn it on as it only had a few dishes in it.

It was definitely about time I went to sleep as the tiredness from waking up a couple of hours earlier still hadn't worn off, so I walked to my room, silently shutting the door behind me.

I got ready for bed, put on my fan, climbed into my bed, and pulled the covers up to my chin.

Tossing and turning, I kept hearing a faint rustling from somewhere. It sounded like paper being squashed. It wasn't until I turned on my side that I realised the sound was coming from under my pillow.

Reaching my hand under, I grasped onto a piece of paper and dragged it out from its hiding spot. Turning on my lamp I quickly read what it said.

My tired brain struggled to comprehend...

This couldn't be happening.

I immediately crumpled up the paper and shoved it into one of my draws, the words written on it replaying over and over in my head so much so that by the time I really started to process what the note meant, the adrenaline had run out and I had drifted off.

We'll be back

CHAPTER 2

After that night, I had trouble sleeping as I kept imagining someone breaking in and hurting me or, worse, mum.

Those disturbing thoughts about who did this, and more importantly, why they did this and what their intentions were, haunted me.

Although I wasn't getting much sleep in the night, I made up for it by going to sleep straight after I came home from school, which mum noticed and commented on, but I brushed it off as the academic year kicking my arse, which to be fair, was.

She was going to be gone from this Friday, so I would be in the house alone. No one was available to come over either so I would have to tough it out on my own.

Every time I walked home from school, I felt like I was being watched. I shook it off and I had got used to it because it had been happening the past week or so. This then made me a bit scared as I considered whether it was the person coming back, but nothing more happened so I had slowly got more and more comfortable.

That was, until one day when I was walking home from school.

It was a normal day apart from the feeling of eyes, but that soon changed, when, out of the corner of my eye, I caught a glimpse of black hair as a person darted around a corner into an alleyway.

Deciding to see what was going on, I walked over to the entrance, peeking around the red brick corner into the dead end.

There was no one there.

Slowly walking to the alley, I didn't see any trace that anyone had been through here, even though I was sure I'd seen someone.

When I got to the end of the alley and I still didn't see anything, I sighed, irritated that my paranoia had made me see things. I turned around to walk back when suddenly, I felt a sense of dread, like the other night, creeping up my spine. This scared me enough that I flew straight out of the alleyway and kept on frantically sprinting until I was nearly home. I only started to slow down when I saw my front door approaching.

Reaching into my pocket for my keys I yanked them out, jammed it into the lock, flung it open before slamming it behind me and double locking it.

I was out of breath. I hated running and that's why I avoided it at all costs - I was definitely feeling the effects now.

Going into the kitchen, I got a glass of water.

I started second guessing myself: was there really someone there? Why didn't I feel anything wrong before I went into the alley?

By the time I'd finished, I was no longer as freaked out as before and chalked the experience down to what had happened last week.

Checking the kitchen counter, I saw the note mum had left.

Have a nice weekend sweetie. I left money on the table xx
Love you.

My mum was always so sweet. I didn't know what I'd do without her.

I was sitting at the kitchen counter thinking about things and made a conscious effort to push my fears away and go to the party that most of my school were going to. With everything that was going on, I really needed a distraction.

Three hours later I was on my way to the party. It didn't take that long to get ready. Luckily, it only took two hours.

I was walking because I didn't want to waste money on an Uber. The money I had was for most meals over the weekend as we had run out of food in the fridge.

When I arrived, I realised that the party was already well underway: beer cans strewn across the front lawn, people standing on the porch drinking and talking and music blaring from inside the house which appeared to shake the whole building.

I walked up the steps, weaving in and out of the people lounging outside.

When I entered the house, the music got even louder and there were way more people, which made me feel quite small and alone. Before anything had even happened, I regretted coming here.

"Watch it!" Some big guy said as I accidentally bumped into him.

Needing to get out of this claustrophobic environment, I hastily darted over to the drinks table, grabbing the first thing I saw and downing it in one gulp.

I grimaced from the taste as I picked up another one, slipping into the less crowded kitchen.

In there, I saw the first person I recognised ... someone I'd forgotten about since the incident.

Blake.

Feeling the courage from the beer, I stepped up to him and patted him on the shoulder. His head turned, but when he saw that it was me, he faced me head on.

"Hey," I said, "how are you?"

"I'm good," he replied, staring at me weirdly. "What are you doing here?"

"Um, at a party, drinking and talking to you."

"I can see that," he said amusingly. "I mean we don't really talk much, do we?"

"No, we don't," I conceded, "but you're the only person I know here is you."

"Oh," he said, frowning, "You didn't come with one of your friends? I always see you with them."

"They were busy and I wanted to have some fun. I didn't expect to see anyone that I knew here, so it's a pleasant surprise." Continuing to look back into the front room.

I wanted to dance.

"...If you need anything, okay?"

"Sure," I said, then downed the rest of my beer. "I'm going to dance." Before slinking away.

Why did I feel so drunk? I had only had two beers.

I decided to check the table where all the drinks had been and then I saw why I felt the way I did.

Someone had spiked the beer with something stronger.

What I wondered was how I hadn't tasted the difference.

It didn't matter, I thought. I wanted to dance.

The rest of the night was a blur of people and drinks. I was dancing and laughing a lot, although I didn't even know who with, which, in my right state of mind, would've scared me, but as I had been drinking a lot it never even crossed my mind once that anything was awry.

"Cops!" Someone in the crowd shouted, breaking me from my trance.

It was a stampede of people running out every exit and as I was pretty drunk, I was having trouble standing up straight in the mob of people.

As I was dragged along with the crowd I stumbled and nearly fell just as someone latched onto my arm, keeping me upright.

"I've got you." They said, before taking me out a different exit as everything faded to black.

The next thing I remembered was waking up in bed with a stranger.

"What the hell!" I shrieked, jumping up and off the bed and falling to the wooden floor. The splitting headache only registered after I had hit the cold boards.

"Just five more minutes," I heard the person, a girl, in the bed mumble before jumping up and staring at me with wide eyes. "Oh, it's just you."

It was Blake's, sister?

Why was I in her bed and how did I get here?

I couldn't remember for the life of me so I decided to ask.

"How the hell did I get here?"

She laughed out loud, "I'm not surprised you don't remember. You were completely trashed last night."

As she said that I started to remember. The hypnotic music, the dancing, the drinking.

"Why did I drink that much?" I groaned and put my hands over my face. "I'm never drinking again."

"That's what they all say." She said with a small chuckle whilst getting up.

"Go and have a shower. You definitely need one right about now." she said, her nose wrinkling before going through her drawer and pulling out some clothes, which she threw to me.

I caught them before going to the bathroom and taking a cold shower. I never coped with hot water very well.

I was putting on the white top and black trousers that Blake's sister had given me when I realised, I didn't even know her name!

As I stepped out, I saw her putting on her uniform for work.

"Hey, I've actually never caught your name."

"Oh, it's Matilda." She said, flashing a smile. "I'm driving to work now; I can drop you on the way there if you want?"

"Thanks, that would be great." I said with a grimace, as my head was still killing me. "Do you have any Ibuprofen? My head feels like it's been kicked in."

"Sure, downstairs in the kitchen. The cupboard above the cooker."

"Thanks," I said, rushing off to quickly get it while also making sure not to jog my head too much. "I appreciate it."

I walked to one end of the hall only to realise that the stairs were at the other end. I definitely should've asked how the hell to even get there as navigation was not my thing.

I reached the kitchen and opened up the cupboard door Matilda had indicated and reached up for the medic's box, but my clumsy ass dropped the thing all over the floor.

"God damnit me." I said under my breath, squatting down to collect all the different kinds of medication.

I saw another hand reach out and grab the ibuprofen off the floor and hand it to me.

It was Blake, who I had forgotten, brought me to his house and stopped me getting in trouble. Either with the stampede, or the police.

Just as I was about to say something he walked over to the other side of the kitchen, opened another cabinet, and pulled some cereal out.

"Hey," I said, quietly. "Thanks for helping me last night."

"I can never resist helping a girl in trouble," He said in a sarcastic tone. "This is my average Saturday; taking drunk girls home and putting them in my sister's room."

I laughed under my breath before standing up and putting the box with all its contents back up in the cupboard.

When I turned around Blake was there with his hand out, a bowl of cereal in it.

I hadn't expected this. I hadn't planned on eating anything before Matilda drove me back.

"Oh," I said, slightly shocked that he'd actually thought of me. "Thank you."

Taking the bowl, I smiled up at him just as our eyes met. He had a gentle look on his face that made my body feel warm.

Wow.

I didn't know that I could have a reaction like that! It had never happened before, but I guess since I was a socially awkward person to strangers it wasn't much of a surprise that I hadn't talked to many boys.

I'd always wanted to have a nice boyfriend and I had met a guy Jessica had set me up on a date with that was interested in me and was exactly my type, but I'd been so nervous that I ended up throwing up in his car...which is usually a mood killer. Unless you're into that. Ew.

I didn't know why I felt less nervous around Blake, but he made me feel like I was special, and I definitely felt more comfortable around him.

I didn't feel like I had to impress him in anyway and that made him special. There was also his good looks and great personality but those were minor parts of his person, obviously.

I had been focused on my food and wasn't really paying attention, so I was surprised to see that when I looked up, Blake was staring at me.

I swallowed my food before speaking.

"I wanted to say thanks," I said nervously, looking down. "I owe you one."

"No." He said, strongly, making me look up. "You don't owe me anything. I did what anyone would do for their friends."

I felt my heart warm at his kind message as I smiled at him, before digging into my food again.

What? I was hungry!

"Well, most friends anyway." He said, quietly.

Startled, I looked up. I thought we had finished our conversation, but I guess not.

"What do you mean?" I asked, curiously.

"Don't drink that much again. I'm not going to be there every time to help you."

I felt like there was something else behind his words. Like he had experienced something bad to do with drinking before or knew someone who had.

"Promise me you won't do it again without having someone there to look out for you."

I wasn't sure why he cared so much, but seeing his concerned face made me instantly want to promise him that I wouldn't.

"I promise."

"It's time to go!" Matilda said, running down the stairs to the front door and interrupting our conversation. I glanced at Blake and saw his head was down and he was focused on his phone.

I got up and started to walk out before turning around and giving Blake a hug.

"Thanks again."

"Don't mention it." He said, smiling lightly.

I got into the passenger side of the car and Matilda drove off.

"So, why were you so drunk and why did Blake bring you back to our house?"

"I may have got wasted," I said, nervously playing with my fingers. "And had no one there to look out for me."

"Well, I'm glad Blake was there. Otherwise, something bad could've happened to you."

She had stopped at a red light and was staring over at me. As I looked at her a weird feeling came over me and I quickly turned away, sunk further into my seat and ignored the mysterious feeling that I felt when I looked into her eyes.

I never knew how to feel about Sundays, because on one hand it was the weekend, I had no school, but on the other, it was also just the day before school started so I had to do any leftover work and go to sleep earlier than either Friday or Saturday.

I had no set time to do my work, so I put it off until later.

I hadn't seen Jill, Hugh or Jessica outside of school in a while so I invited them over as I knew they had nothing to do.

"Hey!" Jill exclaimed hugging me. "It feels like we haven't seen each other outside of school in a while. I'm so glad you called. It was getting boring just sitting in my room all day. Everyone else was staying at Naomi's house and you know I hate that bitch."

I laughed. I always loved how eccentric and vivacious Jill was. She made everything better.

I was suddenly sandwiched into a tight hug.

"Why does Jill get all the attention," Hugh whined. "I'm here too you know?"

I laughed and squeezed him back, then let go and stepped back with a smile.

"Did you bring the thing?" I asked, adding emphasis to 'thing'.

Hugh reached into his massive bag and pulled out four giant gummy Coca-Cola bottles, still in their cardboard packaging.

We'd always talked about getting some massive sweets but hadn't ever gone through with the idea, but for some reason, I felt more confident and had actually got Hugh to buy them for all of us with some of the money I was left for food.

"Yes!" I exclaimed excitedly, snatching one of the boxes out of his hands.

I stared at it in awe as Hugh gave one to Jill and Jessica while keeping one for himself.

We sauntered into the front room carrying extra snacks...crisps, chocolate, the lot.

We sat down and I put on a movie I'd been wanting to watch but hadn't had the chance to until now: Spider-man into the spider-verse. All the reviews I'd seen of it had been extremely good and I was excited about the prospect of not only watching it for the first time, but also having the first-time experience with my best friends as well.

I pressed play on the movie and got comfortable as I ripped open the packaging that was incarcerating my enormous gummy.

I tucked in and enjoyed the movie.

I woke with a start.

Wrappers were strewn all over the table in the middle of the front room and the bowls of crisps were all gone, apart from a few flaky bits at the bottom.

I heard a crash, which startled me, and I looked around at all my friends.

Jessica, Hugh, and Jill were fast asleep.

My heart started to pound, and I felt the need to wake one of them up, so I went over to Jessica and tapped her continually on the shoulder, but no matter how hard I tried, she wouldn't wake up.

Next, I tried Hugh and then Jill. Both ended in the same result.

I heard a quiet creek from upstairs and decided that this time I would be stronger and not let the person get away.

Tiptoeing, I went into the kitchen and grabbed the biggest knife I could find. A 10-inch meat knife was what I came out with, which made me feel more confident.

Slowly, I crept upstairs, making sure to miss all the squeaky parts on the way up.

Moving down the hallway stealthily, I suddenly heard the same sound again. I froze when I heard where it was coming from.

It was coming from my room.

I shook my body and felt the cold burn starting to course through ever cell now that I knew someone was here. The sound being made could only be made by a someone and wouldn't occur on its own!

I also knew that all the people I had invited over were sleeping extremely deeply downstairs; so deeply in fact that I couldn't wake any of them up to come with me so it wasn't any of them.

Mum was also not back yet; she was coming back later today.

I got to the door, pressing my ear against it and listened for a few seconds, which felt like hours, but I didn't hear anything.

Feeling myself calm down I berated my mind for playing tricks on me, but something about the situation still didn't feel right to me so I opened the door cautiously.

At first glance I saw nothing inside. It was empty. It was only when I walked into the room and turned on the light that I was able to analyse everything properly.

My room didn't look much different, but I could tell someone had been inside.

From the rug being moved slightly to the right, to my door stopper being flung to the other side of the room.

As I continued to look silently from the doorway, I heard some movement from outside.

I descended the stairs at a much faster pace than before, but still trying to make as little noise as possible.

When I got into the living room, I saw the Bodyguard book was wide open. When I had left to go upstairs it had been closed and none of my friends were the type of people to play pranks like that.

Quickly, I rushed over to the door, not caring about how much noise I was making now. My heart pounded in my ears as I grabbed the handle of the open door and started to pull it closed when a shadow caught my eye.

Someone was out there.

Watching. Stalking. Waiting.

For what? I could only hope I never found out.

This thought was quickly cut short as I realised that there was someone even closer. Glimpsing the first shadowy figure, I froze, unable to shut the door.

Attempting to rectify my mistake, I pulled as hard as I could on the door, trying to shut it before the person could stop me.

I was too late.

They jammed their hand inside the door before using their other one to forcefully and violently shove it open. They stalked into the room wearing all black, ski masks covering their faces.

I noticed a white rag in their hand, parts of it looking slightly damp. I tried backing away but they lunged and easily grabbed me before I could even move.

The rag was forced over my mouth and nose, and I struggled frantically with every ounce of my strength to get it off while holding my breath, but that plan was futile.

There was no hope, and soon, I drifted into the lonely darkness of unconsciousness.

CHAPTER 3

Jessica

Me and Katie had always been inseparable. We'd had each other's backs since we were six years old and had never looked back since. I wouldn't change our relationship for anything else.

We did most things together as I knew she could get quite nervous, and me being there helped make her feel better, which in turn made me feel better.

When we were nine years old, we went ice skating with our parents. It was Katie's first time but I had skated a lot before and so I showed her how. She was a great learner and caught on quickly so it was no surprise when she was up and skating within half an hour of me helping her.

The downfall here was Katie's constant want for overachievement. She never gave up and didn't stop doing something until it was perfect.

She tried more and more extravagant moves until she did one wrong, and fell, hitting her chin on the ice, gaining a cut. Her chin needed cleaning and then a plaster, but she wouldn't allow her mum or my parents to do it for her as she only wanted me to. They showed me the best way and I cleaned it and put a cute blue plaster onto her chin.

After this we went back to skating, her being more careful and sticking closer to me while I made sure to keep a closer eye on her.

That incident made us closer than ever and from that day on, she always stayed closer to me whenever I was around.

Which is why I was surprised she was nowhere in the house when we all woke up.

We checked all the bedrooms, the bathroom, the closets and even the basement and garden; but she was nowhere to be seen.

I wasn't too worried as she sometimes liked to go off on her own to think so it didn't bother me when I found her phone on the shelf next to the back door. When she went out, she liked to go without it so she wouldn't have any distractions.

"She's probably meeting some hot guy," Jill said. "And who wouldn't want to date her? She's sexy!"

I made a non-committal sound, not believing that to be true, before standing up to leave. I made sure to grab Kate's phone before as the first thing she always did when she came back was come to me.

I got in my car and turned it on, putting on the radio before driving off.

I arrived home very quickly, parked my car, and went inside. I snuck in as I wanted to avoid mum, but as I was going up the stairs, I realised she had told me she wasn't going to be home today, and I felt my body slump in relief.

Going into my room I took Katie's phone out, trying to turn in on.

Unsurprisingly, it wasn't charged so I got my charger out and plugged it in, leaving it on my bedside table.

I went downstairs and put on some food. Rice and chicken was always a good option.

While the chicken was cooking and before I put on the rice, I put the TV on, not really paying attention to what was on.

When my food was done, I turned off the TV and decided to go upstairs and watch the TV there.

Opening my door, I remembered about Katie's phone and decided to check it.

I typed in her pin and it opened.

I knew that she liked to take pictures so the first course of action would be to check her gallery.

Weird. The first few pictures were of darkness. I couldn't really make out anything, so I turned up the brightness and leaned in closer to the screen.

To say what I saw on the screen shocked me would be an understatement.

It was a picture of someone in a black mask waving at the camera and it freaked me out.

Unfortunately, that wasn't the scariest part. What terrified me more, was that the person had a knife in their hand.

I swiped to the next picture and let out a gasp, immediately muffled by my hand.

There were pictures of us sleeping from last night taken from outside the house and in the reflection of the glass door you could now see two people in masks.

I swiped to the next picture and a cold fear took over my body.

It was Katie, but she wasn't awake. She had tape over her mouth and her hands were bound with rope tightly. I could see the rope burns on her wrists, which must've come from shifting in her unconscious state.

I quickly stood up and rushed downstairs, putting my shoes on before getting in my car, quickly backing out of the driveway and then speeding to the police station - I didn't care - I needed to get there fast.

While driving, I was having trouble with steering as my hands were shaking so much. I was scared and fearful over what potentially had happened to Katie, and I didn't know how to deal with it.

When I arrived, I parked on some double yellow lines before hopping out and power walking into the station. I talked to someone, and they calmed me down, took the evidence and helped me file a police report.

Afterwards, as I was still quite freaked out, I sat in my car and thought about what could've happened to her. I quickly pulled out my own phone. I needed to call Kate's mum, Lila.

I dialled her number and waited.

"Hello?" I head a tired voice say, as papers shuffled in the background.

"Lila? It's me, Jessica," I said, my voice shaking a bit. "Katie is missing."

That fully woke her up.

"What?!" She said, loudly, sounding like she was suddenly moving stuff around in the room. "What do you mean she is missing?"

"I found pictures on her phone," I said, choking up at the images painfully rooted in my mind. "Two people in black, and they were carrying her while she was sleep."

"I'm coming back, I'll be there soon." She said quickly, the noises becoming more frantic.

"Bye...call me when you land." I said, before the line went dead, and I put my phone back in my pocket.

I felt void, hopeless that I could do nothing to help.

I really hoped that this wasn't the last time I would see Katie again. I definitely knew that I wouldn't be able to live with that.

CHAPTER 4

Katie

I woke up with a start; I couldn't see anything. I felt something covering my face and tried to reach up to remove it but found that my hands were tied behind my back.

I started panicking and thrashing around. I didn't know what was happening.

"Hey, shut it!" I heard a booming voice from right next to me before I felt a blow to my side. The wind was knocked out of me and I started coughing. I stopped thrashing because I was scared of getting hit again.

What the hell was going on?!

I heard the person standing next to me walk away and they started talking to someone else a bit further away.

"...not ready yet..." I could only make out bits and pieces as they were talking quietly.

"...doesn't matter...boss wants her ready...rigorous training courses..." I was straining my ears a great deal to hear the small snippets of conversation.

"Get her ready. The Mamba is in position."

I didn't know what the Mamba was, but I definitely did not like it at all. I heard the person move closer to me and I tried escaping from their grasp by wiggling but they slapped me across the face, dazing me.

"Stay still, otherwise I'll hurt you more." They said in a strangely calm tone that instantly made me cease my struggling.

The man dragged me up by my arms and roughly walked me to wherever it was that he was taking me.

By the time we stopped, I didn't have a clue where we could be as there had been so many twists and turns along the way, resulting in me being even more distressed.

The smell of the place was horrible. The metallic stench, only cut by something that reminded me of vinegar, invaded my nostrils and gave my system a massive shock. It was horrid.

"Don't try to run," The man's wet breath encased my ear as he whispered, gripping my arms even tighter before continuing in a louder voice. "Do you understand?"

I vigorously nodded my head hoping that he wouldn't do anything else to me. Luckily, to my relief, he untied my wrists and removed my blind fold.

The fear that had left me quickly took hold again as I saw the scene in front of me.

A girl, a few years older than me, stared at me like she hated me, like she wanted to kill.

She was wearing a tank top so I could see old scars mingled with fresh cuts covering her body. Angry bruises covered her face as well.

"I'm going to enjoy this." The man who had been leading me said, as he walked away and out the door before shutting and locking it.

As soon as the door was shut the girl started to advance on me.

"Wait! What are you doing?" I cried out, trying to get her to stop, "Please!"

She didn't stop and the first punch that connected with my side felt like it broke a few ribs.

I cried out and stumbled to the side, putting my arms up to block the next punch, but she saw this and kicked me hard in the knee.

My legs crumbled from under me as an excruciating pain emanated from my knee. I glanced down at it and through my tears, saw that it was bent at a weird angle.

The girl grabbed me by my hair and dragged me to my feet. I hopped along after her, desperate to keep my knee from getting hit by anything else.

But that turned out to be the least of my worries.

The beating took what felt like hours and the majority of my bones were broken by the time she was finished. I couldn't move without experiencing pain that I didn't even know was possible to feel.

"That's enough, Mamba." I heard someone from the door say and she instantly backed away from me.

It didn't stop the constant agony or my sobbing though.

I felt a needle enter my neck and I blacked out.

I slowly woke in a nice bed. I tried to move but experienced the worst pain I've ever felt before and then it all came back to me.

I looked around, as my neck felt bruised and battered but not broken, and saw a someone standing by the door. My breathing started to quicken and swallowing was nearly impossible before the person stepped into the light and I saw they were wearing a white lab coat.

It was then that I took in the rest of my surroundings and saw that I was in a hospital, although, as I focused my hearing, I couldn't hear anyone else, but I shook that off.

"Ms. Bloom?" I heard the doctor say. I turned my head to face him, careful to keep my body from moving. "You're awake, good."

I didn't know what it was about him but my feelings of dread suddenly shot off the scale. Unfortunately, I couldn't voice any of those thoughts as I had a breathing tube in my mouth that was probably going to get taken out as I was awake now.

"It seems you've had a bit of an incident," the doctor said with a straight face. "Looks like you really don't know anything about fighting. We should have waited for a while before letting the Mamba have a go at you."

My eyes bulged and I gagged on the tube. He knew the people who took me and was helping them!

My eyes burned with bitter tears as I was, unable to do anything, at his mercy.

"You're probably wondering why I'm helping those people that took you," he said with a light chuckle, as he walked closer to me. "I have a bit of a confession to make."

He leaned closer to me and whispered in my ear. "I was the one who took you." He laughed maniacally, standing back up.

I started full on crying now, the sobs racking my body making me cry out in pain.

"No need to cry Ms. Bloom," He said, walking about the room. "You're in safe hands now."

A woman walked in and brought out a needle before injecting it into the bag of fluids attached to me. It wasn't long before whatever she injected went through the cannula and into my body.

I was out cold before I even knew what had happened.

I woke up with a pounding headache. It was so bad that it felt like my head would split open. I guess I did have space available for another type of pain.

Someone was sitting in a chair near me, but by this time I was in too much pain and too exhausted to really care anymore.

"If you're going to kill me, just do it already." I said, my flat voice barely audible with how dry my throat was.

"Why would we want to kill you?" A woman's voice answered as she got up from the chair and walked over to me. "You're our newest recruit."

Recruit? For what?

My mind boggled by that revelation and I struggled to understand why they would choose me and if I was their recruit, why would they do this to me and what were they recruiting me for?

"Why wouldn't we want you? You have exactly what we look for in a new recruit," Despite the swelling and bruising, she must've seen the confusion on my face because she stroked my numb cheek and said, "Although, your fighting technique is something that we really need to improve fast."

Fighting?

I didn't know how to fight. I'd never got into a fight before and I had never taken any fighting lessons before.

What was I even being recruited to? If my earlier experience of being battered had anything to do with what they did, I wanted nothing to do with them.

My thoughts were interrupted as a smartly dressed man walked into the room holding a clipboard, making me realise that the woman had left the room

"Good evening Ms. Bloom," So it was later in the day than I had thought. "I'm your assigned doctor until you've recovered from your injuries."

He walked over to me, clipboard in hand and got his pen ready.

"Can you tell me where the pain is." He said with a stunning smile.

I didn't see any other choice and maybe he could even help me. So, I answered him.

"Everywhere." My raspy voice was unrecognisable to my own ears.

"And where is the pain the worst?"

I thought for a minute, analysing where the main source of pain was before telling him that it was my knee, in an even weaker voice.

"Lastly, how much do you know about what we're doing here?"

I managed a subtle shake of my head, which he correctly interpreted as me not knowing anything other than they had kidnapped me and hurt me badly.

"Well, you see Ms. Bloom," He started, "The organisation I work for specialises in training young girls to become cold blooded killers."

"Additionally," He said, walking around the room with his hands resting on the small of his back. "The world is a very dangerous place, which I'm sure you already know, and someone has to keep everything in order. Things like making sure the right person gets into power or that no one is spilling any, very, classified secrets. This organisation, for example."

An assassination organisation...

'Why me specifically' I wanted to ask, but couldn't force the words out of my distorted mouth.

"You must be wondering why we picked you and not other girls who might be more qualified." I was surprised that he could tell the basis of my thoughts. "Now I don't know who, but someone high up in our organisation has said that you would be a great recruit as you're truly good. Which always means that once broken you'll be truly bad."

I didn't feel anything anymore except the tears welling up in my eyes. I tried to blink them away but failed. Soon, my cheeks were covered in salty tears that got into every cut and I could barely see anymore.

"Hmm." I heard the man mutter, "You're going to be a fun one to break."

A bitter chill rolled up my spine and the delicate hunger that was beginning to surface vanished. I felt sick. Before I could even think about trying to move, he was above me with a needle in his hand.

I looked on in fear as he got it ready.

"This is my best creation yet," He said in awe. "It makes certain parts of the parietal lobe fire at excessive rates, putting the human body in an excruciating amount of pain for hours on end. I've always wanted to try it out on a person already in pain."

He said all this in a calm voice, just as when he had seemed to care for me, which is what made this that much scarier.

"I'm going to have fun with this." He muttered under his breath before injecting me with the concoction.

The pain I felt in that moment surpassed any other I had felt before, including the torture at the hands of the Mamba.

My memory, for some time, was extremely hazy as I had been going in and out of consciousness due to the unbearable pain.

Sometimes, I'd get a glimpse of a girl next to my bed, although I couldn't make anything out apart from her red hair, before I was pulled under again.

I released a groan as I came to, surprised that a lot of the pain was gone. Even my throat was no longer as dry.

"Hello." I heard from my right, startlingly me.

I turned as quickly as my body allowed me, only to come face to face with a girl who had red hair.

Just like what I had seen while on the mixture of drugs.

I stared at her and she did the same to me. We both studied each other. Me, because I hadn't seen another person around my age in here and her, well, I could only guess what horrible thoughts she was having if she was anything like any of the other people here.

"I brought you something," She said, putting a tray on my lap and a fork in my hand that I now realised was no longer in a cast. "Can you sit up?"

"No." I said, being unintentionally short with her.

"Let me help you with that." She said, before gently leaning me forward and then moving the back of the bed up so it rested behind me again.

I gave her a nod, my voice already feeling kind of weak.

I started eating straight away, forcing food in my mouth quickly, only now realising how hungry I was.

I heard a small laugh beside me and glanced at the redhead to see that she had a small smile on her face.

I wasn't embarrassed like I would usually have been. I had gone through so much already that this was nothing. I just went back to eating in exactly the same way.

She moved her chair back and headed towards the door so I quickly finished my mouthful as I still didn't know who she was.

"Who are you?" I asked, just as she had opened the door.

She stopped right in the doorway and looked back at me. "I'm Drew, your partner."

Partner?

I didn't dwell on it though as I had enough questions about my situation to last a life time and I didn't think I was getting any of them answered any time soon.

My broken bones had been healing very well over the past few weeks, although I couldn't tell exactly how many had pasted.

Drew came into my room sometimes and we talked but every time I brought up anything to do with me being kidnapped, she seemed to shut down. After a while I stopped asking her those questions, and instead, I talked to her like a normal person.

"Really? You can do 50 pull ups?" I scoffed in disbelief.

"Of course." She said. "All of us can."

I stayed clear of asking any questions about who 'all' of us were but it didn't stop my mind racing through possibilities.

Our conversation was interrupted by a man who slammed the door open and shouted something at Drew in another language.

Her answer seemed to anger him more as he started to turn red before gesturing out the room and then Departing hastily, leaving the door open.

"I have to go." She said in a cold, weary tone. "I'll see you tomorrow."

"Wait!" I said, making her pause. "Who was that?"

"Leave it alone Katie." She said, her voice all of a sudden taking on a tired characteristic before she slipped out the door, leaving me to my own thoughts.

I was now always conscious of my surroundings. Them torturing me over the course of those weeks made me aware of all my surroundings and more alert to any sort of threats.

So, when I had quiet weeks like the past few, I got more and more nervous that someone would hurt me again. They hadn't done anything for a while, but my anxiety wasn't going anywhere.

While here, I remembered some of the things I had read online about what to do in a situation like this. The top one was - always stay calm and analyse the situation. Look for details that can help later on and make sure to always stay alert to any potential danger - which was what I was doing and, I think, doing well.

Even though I was calm and collected on the outside, inside, I was freaking out. Lately I had even been having trouble controlling it.

I'd been fucking kidnapped and tortured by some people who were forcibly recruiting me into their organisation full of assassins?

This was my worst nightmare, like something from a horror movie.

"Hello again." The woman said, walking through the door. "I see you're recovering well."

She indicated my arms in much less restrictive positions.

It was the woman who explained what the organisation was about and what they wanted with me.

I wasn't sure if I was actually afraid of her, but my heart didn't care as it was beating so loudly. I was worried she would be able to hear it.

"I'm Dr. Rodriguez and I'm here to do a psychological evaluation on you to make sure everything we observed was correct," She said in a matter-of-fact tone. "Make sure to answer correctly, otherwise you'll face the consequences of your actions."

If I wasn't scared before, I most certainly was now.

"How are you feeling about getting..." She paused, seemingly looking for the right word. "Taken."

She said I had to be truthful, and I didn't want to face the consequences of not doing what I was told, so I followed her orders.

"I'm scared, annoyed and anxious. I don't want to be here and just want to go home." By the end I was pleading.

She wrote something down, ignoring my last sentence.

"How are you getting along with Drew so far?" She asked, staring me straight in the eye.

The cold and calculated look in them frightened me and actually helped me regain my composure.

"Drew has helped me a lot with recovering," I said, not wanting to get Drew in trouble by over sharing. "I feel a lot better every time she's with me."

She looked content with my answer and I sighed in relief. At least this looked like it was going well.

"How would you feel about us sending someone to kill all your family and friends?"

What?

Why the hell was she asking this question?

Were they going to do it if I didn't give the right response? Or had they already done it and wanted to know my reaction to it.

Before I could even answer I heard her speak.

"That's what we were looking for." she said, writing something down.

"What do you mean?" I asked, having found the courage to speak in a semi-normal tone.

"I was wondering if you were going to lie to us. By the end of the program you won't care about any of your family or friends, but right now, unfortunately, you do and your face showed panic, which is a valid response in this moment." She explained, giving me a cruel smile.

I took in the words she said and felt a massive sense of relief. My family weren't dead and no one was looking to kill them if I cooperated.

She asked a few more questions that, by analysing them properly, I inferred that they were to do with my mental health and if I was going to have any side effects from the "incidents" from before.

I answered accordingly but also embellished the truth a little as I knew she would know if I was lying. I knew the consequences of doing nothing so I didn't want to imagine what they'd do if I actually did something that they didn't like.

"That's all Ms. Bloom. Thank you for cooperating." She said, a tight smile on her face, before turning around and exiting the room. Her heels clicked down the corridor and faded away from me.

I felt muscles that I didn't know I was clenching release as she got further and further away, until I couldn't hear her anymore.

Everything around here was dangerous and no matter what, I was not letting my guard down. I couldn't let them break me. I needed to get back to the people I loved and stop whatever this 'organisation' was from hurting anyone I knew.

I probably wouldn't be able to make a difference but as long as I kept my family safe, I didn't care what happened to me.

I felt rejuvenated, which was a complete change from the last few weeks where I didn't really care if I lived or died.

I would do whatever it took to take down all these people running the organisation, or I would die trying.

"Alright new recruits, get into a straight line," Dr. Rodriguez, whose first name I had heard from the chatter of others, as Ana, demanded. "Quickly now, we don't want to have to make you."

Ana seemed like one of the higher ups. She was constantly ordering others around and was the one other people went to if they needed help.

None of the students dared to though. They seemed too scared and I definitely understood why.

"First we have two hours of jogging," She said, pointing at the indoor track that already had a few kids running around it. "Then we move onto fifty squats, thirty push ups, twenty pull ups and we finish off with three hours in the rooms."

I looked around me at all the kids as they shuffled nervously, some playing with their fingers and crossing their feet while others looked at the ground, clearly scared.

"Just remember, once we start you can't stop, otherwise you'll regret it." She said, in a tone like this was normal and expected.

A girl near the front chuckled. "What are you going to do about it. There are more of us that you so you can't make us do anything."

I heard some of the other girls grow louder as they latched onto this girl's confidence. But not me. Not after what I had been through.

They didn't understand that they would actually have something horrible done to them if they didn't comply. The fact that they hadn't experienced the pain I had or the utter despair I had felt for weeks made me feel very jealous, but those thoughts were quickly washed away as Ana started talking again.

Her eyes scanned over the children, seemingly taking note of who was opposing her and who wasn't questioning her decision before she came to a conclusion.

"Put the girl up." She said, apparently to no one. It was only then that I noticed five people with masks on dropping out of the shadows. The others saw it a little after me and quietened down, losing all the confidence they had built up.

They grabbed the girl, four holding her to make sure she couldn't move one bit while the other tied her hands above her head. They then dragged her over to a chain hanging from the ceiling and wrapped it around the rope that tied her hands together.

She was kicking and thrashing so they bound her legs as well, making sure that she wasn't a threat any longer.

I was scared about what they were going to do and wasn't sure if she'd still be alive by the end of it. I didn't want to see any person die in front of me.

Three girls without masks walked out with tape around their hands and blank looks on their faces. They looked a little older than me but still very young.

"You may go." Ana said to the masked figures.

They nodded and vanished back into the shadows, leaving the room, although their menacing presence loomed.

"Now, make sure you watch closely because this will be you if you don't listen to exactly what I'm saying." She said, standing next to the girl who had now frozen up and gone sheet white.

The three people that had entered before suddenly surrounded her and waited for Dr. Rodríguez's commanded.

"Begin." She said with a calm and loose tone, seeming to perk up from the display that was about to happen.

The girls started hitting the strung-up kid hard, aiming only for the gut. Some of the girls were in shock while others looked like they were about to cry. The pained cries from the beaten girl were very hard to listen to.

The beating continued and the girl suddenly threw up all over the floor, her puke a touch red from blood.

I felt a strange feeling of satisfaction wash over me. I was glad that someone else was going to experience even a fraction of my pain. If I had to deal with it then others should as well.

These thoughts went as quickly as they came and I was left feeling a bit confused about them so I shook myself and ignored it.

The cries and screams had vanished and all that was left was the sounds of the grunts from the girls and of their fists hitting the girl in the stomach.

After what felt like ages Ana got the three girls to leave.

"This will be you if you don't comply," She said, her menacing glance scouring across all of us. "Never, ever question my power."

She suddenly turned around and undid the chain holding the girl up and she flopped onto the ground; out cold.

The others stood in shocked silence. They obviously hadn't expected anything like this, as if this kind of violence was foreign to real life violence because they were seeing it with their own eyes. Like me before I arrived here.

Ana walked out gesturing for us to follow. A heavy silence descended over the whole group as we left the bare room, leaving the poor girl a beaten mess upon the floor.

We walked down the corridor, the boots that they gave us being the only sound made. We walked until we reached the end of the corridor and then followed Ana inside the door.

"Listen up," She said in a calm tone with a sinister smile. "We are going to start your training now, and don't complain as we don't want another incident now, do we?"

Everyone remained quiet and didn't dare to utter a word.

"Good!" she said as her whole person changed into a more cheerful one. "Now get to it. We haven't got all day."

Training was intense. More intense than any other thing I'd done in my life before.

I had a bit of experience with running and as I was able to choose my speed I didn't struggle too much. When it came to the other things, however, I struggled quite a lot. I was very lucky that some of the people that were training with me every session were very unfit and were struggling to do any of the training.

You might have wondered why I was so calm. I also wondered that. After I thought I was going to die I hadn't really cared much for anything. I liked my chats with Drew but I didn't really get the same overall enjoyment out of life like I did before. I felt less emotional and didn't react anymore to the violence constantly going on around me.

Since the start of my time here I felt much more physically capable of many different things. I was able to run for longer, I was stronger, I was quicker and felt that my senses were more in tune with the rest of my body. I over all felt better, physically, and mentally.

We hadn't trained in fighting yet but I was sure I could give someone a real fight because of my speed and ability to quickly analyse and adapt to situations, even in the tensest moments. This was something I hadn't had before I was taken.

"So," Drew said, breaking me from my thoughts. "How is your training going?"

I had expected everyone at the higher levels to know how all of our training was proceeding but it seemed that information was something Ana wanted to keep private. She had her reasons and neither I or anyone else was willing to risk her wrath by asking.

"I'm much more toned," I said pulling up my shirt to show the starting definition of abs. "Although I am more mentally tired each day. It's much harder work that I thought."

"Yeah, it was like that for me when I first started," She said, in her own world. "Before..."

She trailed off and seemed to get lost in her own thoughts so I tapped her on the shoulder and she quickly snapped out of it and flashed me a smile.

"Sorry, I completely zoned out." She said with a small chuckle, scratching the back of her neck.

She obviously didn't want to stay on this subject so I changed it and we just talked about life. I could see the relief on her face even though she tried to hide it.

"Well, I'd better get going." Drew said, standing up and turning to leave.

She quickly patted my shoulder as she walked passed me and then out of my room and into the dim hallway to her room, which was a short distance from mine.

"Bye." I said, unconsciously smiling.

When Drew had told me she was the partner that I had, at first I assumed she'd be my roommate too but once I healed and got to my room and only saw a small concrete box with one bed, I knew that it was me alone at night.

A lot of people had different theories that could be heard as you walked into the food hall or when we were all going back to our rooms.

The most popular between the girls here was that they didn't want anyone forming real relationships, but as they allowed people to go into each other's rooms anytime in the day, it didn't look like that was the case at all to me.

What I thought was that they wanted you to get used to the lonely feeling of sleeping by yourself without anyone to talk to or just to have there as a comfort. It made sense to me, as being able to isolate yourself from your surroundings was a trait most people didn't have and so it was no surprise that they'd do this.

However, they didn't want us to feel helpless and completely alone. They wanted us to also bond with our partners so that whatever we did together, we'd have good chemistry and be able to spend days with each other without annoyance to the point of abandoning the other. I had heard rumours of that happening and the abandoner ended up dying, but that's just a rumour.

Figuring out a way out of here was something I didn't think about as the few who I had seen try were tortured before they were killed. It was all put on display to make us docile and scare us into submission, and it worked. No one had tried after the first few weeks as the final kid's execution was put on display in front of everybody.

Her brutal beheading was still embedded in my mind and nothing I did could remove it. I had told Drew some of what happened and she told me that what happened was normal and to be expected. By the tone of her voice I could tell there was more to it, but as I didn't trust her and didn't want to become a nuisance and annoy her, I didn't bother. I never got around to expressing my feelings on how much the situation really affected me. Right now, all I could do was train and hope that someday I would get a great opportunity to escape. In the meantime, I had to fall in line and wait. I was no use to myself, my friends or family if I was dead.

CHAPTER 5

We'd been training for a few months now and we were almost at the stage where we would start the real fights. Every time I thought about it, I felt a strange jolt of excitement before nerves took over and I'd go back to being scared again.

I had got a lot of information about Drew and her time here, had built a bond with her as she was the only one I hadn't had any hostile interactions with and was also the only one who, as much as I hated to say it, I was actually starting to care about.

"So, how are you feeling about the fights?" Drew asked, leaning back and relaxing on the bed beside me.

"Nervous." I released in a breath.

After an incident in the food room where I had accidentally spilt some food on the main clique of girls who always hung around together, she was the one who helped to calm them down and make sure that I was safe. After that, I couldn't deny that she at least was looking out for me, even if I didn't know the intentions behind it.

"Just remember that I'm always here for you if you need me." She said, taking my hand and squeezing it.

"I won't." I replied, turning towards her and smiling while squeezing her hand back.

The warm feeling she gave me reminded me of my friends at home. Sudden sadness wash over me as I thought about all my friends; especially my best friend Jessica. I really missed her. I had been able to go to her whenever I wanted for anything I needed, if it was just to talk, to cuddle up when it was cold, or just sitting next to each other. It was all missing from my life right now and was one of the only things keeping my motivated carry on in this place.

"You'll be fine." She murmured as I fell asleep.

"Begin!" Ana's voice boomed out as we got into fighting stances, sizing each other up.

I'd been partnered with a girl around my size who still looked pretty scared after all her time here. I was glad I wasn't partnered with one of the bigger girls because even with the training we'd been receiving for the last few weeks, I didn't think I could compete with their raw strength.

It had been two weeks since we had started and luckily, I hadn't been used as a demonstration yet, but if I was lacking it wouldn't be long until I was. Ana thought using actual humans would give a much better representation of how the scenario would go in real life, which I agreed with. I just didn't want to be the one demonstrated on.

Fighting had always been something I'd wanted to be good at but never bothered getting into. Those factors, despite with the fact that I had no choice, resulted in me getting some joy out of it and improving at an alarming rate. Even faster than I normally would.

Some might think me cruel for ignoring the girls who got used as training dummies but that's how life worked here and we all had to either deal with it or suffer the consequences and I knew which one I'd rather.

We'd been trained to look for people's weaknesses and think on our feet of ways to exploit them. I used this to my advantage and studied my opponent fast, searching for any weak points. I didn't want to give her any time to descend on me. Observing her legs, I noticed how she kept one leg straightened more than the other, so I quickly pounced on the opportunity and faked high with a punch and while she went to block that, I kicked her in her exposed leg. She let out a cry of pain and fell to the floor. I waited for Ana to come over as I didn't want to do anything I wasn't supposed to do. After checking on some of the other people, she walked over looking at the scene before her.

"Good job," She said, making no move to help the girl or make sure she was alright. "You're one of our brightest students."

Hearing that from her made a feeling of warmth surge though my veins and I stood a bit straighter.

"Thank you." I said, in as confident a voice as possible.

She nodded and then told me as she left to help the girl up and check if she was okay. I didn't really care as I knew she would've done the same to me if she'd had the chance, but I didn't want to make enemies cause in here, they were almost guaranteed to hurt you or your friends.

When I saw the indignant look on her face as she stood up, I felt a jolt in my stomach and a smile started to slither onto my face but I quickly suppressed those feelings and carried on as if nothing had ever happened.

"Let me know if you need any help." I said to the girl, already walking away before I heard her answer.

We were told to go to the office once we had finished our training and wait outside till we were called in. None of us knew what the hell we were going to do, or what was going on and that scared us. I tried not to show it but some were not as successful as me because they looked as if they were about to cry.

"Next." I heard from the office.

I hadn't expected it to be my turn this quickly as none of the girls had come back out yet and the time had passed super-fast.

I walked up to the door and felt a cleanness wash over me, replacing my nerves. I opened the door and stepped inside, ready to see what was needed of me.

"Your score is 98 out of 100." I heard coming from all around me. There must have been speakers. "You passed. You can carry on with your training."

I felt excited that I had done something right and didn't have to worry about the potential consequences I would've faced I had done badly.

"Exit through the door on your left. You're ready for the next step." The voice said, almost mechanically, like it had done this hundreds of times before and it was now routine. "You'll be training for your first mission so be prepared."

My first mission?

I knew that this organisation trained girls to be killers but was I ready for that?

I didn't know, and frankly, I didn't have to worry about it as I knew that Ana and the higher ups wanted the best girls to succeed so they'd give them as good a chance as possible.

So, while I didn't know if I was ready, I was damn sure going to try and get there.

The equipment that was laid out in front of me was like you'd see in a movie. Guns, knives, swords, daggers, and some gadgets that looked harmless but I was sure were able to end lives as easily as all the other weapons.

End lives? What was I thinking? I was not a killer and I would never be...? If I could survive what they did to me when they first took me, they would never be able to break me.

Although I was going to avoid trying to kill anyone as much as possible, I knew that it wasn't always that simple. On missions, we were expected to kill people or take them out by other means. Sometimes other people could get in the way of the job, and I might be forced to take them out to save my own life.

I wasn't going to actively look for ways to kill and would rather take a harder option because it was less deadly. Which is why, when asked what weapon I wanted, I chose the double daggers as they were small, easily concealable and didn't always have to be lethal, unlike a gun. The chance of killing someone by shooting them almost anywhere in the body was extremely high and I didn't want to risk doing that. I also trusted my own body so I could control the swings of the knives, gauge how deep the cuts were and how much force I used, compared to a gun being fired. Once a bullet was fired no one could stop it without special means, which most people didn't have.

"Daggers are different to the swords we've trained you with so far. You have to get much closer to your target, which is much trickier." One of the many different coaches said as she flipped a dagger in her hand. "You have to be sure, otherwise you'll be useless in the field and nothing more than dead weight."

"I'm sure." I said confidently. We had a book we had to read on the aspects of getting close to your target to either kill them or take them down as you couldn't always use a long-ranged weapon - some jobs required more finesse and grace. These could only be provided with a human touch.

"Good, we'll begin the actual training on using your chosen weapon later today as you still have to carry on your combat practise," She said, putting the daggers away in a small black bag. "You better be fully focused, otherwise you're going to get seriously hurt."

Even though I was confident that I could quickly adapt to using a dagger it didn't stop my heart from quickening at the thought of fighting with a knife where the most injury could be caused in the least amount of time. I wasn't sure if I was ready to go into full fights with something I'd never used, but I had no choice. I had to do it no matter what.

I flopped onto my bed making sure to keep my arms off of it so they didn't hurt as much. I had finished all my training for today and the main technique that was focused on was blocking blows from other people with knives. I wasn't very good at it at first and had ended up with loads of cuts going up and down my arms. I knew Drew was going to come to my room later and because I'd told her I had chosen a dagger, she mentioned that she would bring bandages; without me asking. I wasn't even thinking of that before the training so I was glad she had.

My end goal still hadn't changed as I was always looking for ways to escape this place, but my heart wasn't in it as much as before because I had found nothing that could help me or had any opportunity to break out of here. This didn't mean that I wasn't trying. I was. It just meant that I didn't have many options left. My best option would be on a mission. On a missions we're under minimal surveillance as they only send out the required amount of people to that certain location.

I had almost told Drew of my plans a few times but chickened out because I was scared of her reaction.

Would she be happy? Angry? Or would she turn me in and tell Dr Rodriguez that I was planning to escape? I couldn't risk it until I was more confident about my plan and Drew.

I heard my door open and then shut.

"I'm here," Drew said, then gestured towards the tin in her hands. "And I brought the kit."

"Thanks. You're a life saver."

I took my top off so the cuts could be accessed more easily.

"Damn," Drew let out a low whistle. "When I first did my training, it wasn't close to this bad."

I looked down at my arms and properly saw them for the first time. Cuts and scratches enveloped my forearms. Some deep, some shallow but all varying in sizes.

"I take it you weren't very good?" Drew joked.

Taking out some cotton wool and coating it with a liquid from a brown bottle, she turned towards me and gently grasped my arm.

"This is going to sting a little." She said just before she pressed it on my wounds.

It only stung a little, surprisingly enough. I thought it would hurt more because when people usually say that line, it ends up being very painful.

"You're dealing with this well." Drew said, surprised that I wasn't reacting at all.

"I've had worse." I replied, not really wanting to say anymore on the matter.

Drew finished cleaning my cuts and went on to bandage my arms up nice and securely.

"There we go. Done," She said, patting me on the back. "That went way better than my first time. I cried like a little bitch."

I let out a laugh at the sudden outburst as I hadn't expected anything like that to come out of her mouth.

"Well yeah, of course you'd act like that. You're you." I said, raising an eyebrow with a slight smirk on my face.

"Oh, grow up." Drew said, pushing me lightly.

She glanced at the watch on her hand before looking towards me. By her look alone I knew that she needed to go.

"Bye Drew." I said hugging her. "Thanks for all the help."

"Of course, what else are friends for." She replied, her hand waving goodbye as she walked towards the door. "Bye Kate."

She vanished into the hallway leaving me alone.

I let out a massive yawn and suddenly the day hit me. I hadn't realised I was this tired but it shouldn't have been a surprise after all the intense training. I got into bed and fell asleep as soon as my head hit the pillow.

I had steadily been improving my knife skills over the last couple of training sessions to where I was actually able to block most of the blows, only getting cut a few times.

The cuts I was getting, although probably more severe, didn't seem to hurt as much, which I took as a good sign.

I was getting better and I could not only see the results, I could feel them.

My reaction time felt a lot quicker; my hand eye coordination was much better and I was actually very good at dodging hits from knife fights. Even to the extent where the instructor had a hard time hitting me.

I had started to feel excited for my training sessions.

Excited to improve my hand eye coordination.

Excited to hone my ability and become a good blade wielder.

I was looking forward to all of this and couldn't wait until I was good enough so that the teacher would struggle and maybe even be forced to concede. I knew I could get that good.

Of course, it would take a lot of hard work and dedication, but I was willing to put that in as the results spoke for themselves.

I didn't have much time to dwell on my thoughts as I had to get to the main hall quickly. We all had letters left on our beds telling us to come to the main hall at four in the afternoon and it was five to right now. Drew hadn't given anything away, although she seemed relatively excited about whatever it was.

I got to the door of the main hall and walked inside, seeing almost everyone already there. I knew the other girls weren't going to be late though. We couldn't afford to be when in a place like this. I hadn't bothered making any friends here as I didn't need anyone else but Drew and myself. If I had other people, they would just be a distraction; unnecessary interferences. So, I held off and kept to myself. By the allotted time everyone had arrived and no sooner had that occurred, Dr Rodriguez walked into the room, confident and uncaring. She seemed to be more focused on the tablet in her hand.

We quietly waited for a few minutes while she finished up whatever she was doing.

"Now," Dr Rodriguez said. "The reason you've been ordered here is because you're all going to be going on your first missions within the month."

The silence got quieter, if that were even possible, and no one seemed to know what to do.

"Good, I'm glad you're all taking this well," Although her words may have appeared to be kind, I could definitely see from her smirk that she understood how we were all feeling and revelled in that fact. "You're going to come up one by one and get your assigned mission. This is a solo mission, so everything is on you." She looked around the room with her piercing gaze. "We don't accept failure."

I let her cold words wash over me, using them as motivation to work as hard as possible so I didn't fail. I would do anything to succeed. Anything.

One by one we went up, collecting the location of the place we were traveling to and before I knew it, it was my turn.

I walked up and was about to walk back when I felt a hand grip my arm and I froze.

"You'll get to talk to your partner and they'll give you directions and help you out." Dr Rodriguez said, squeezing my arm tighter. "Don't fail. You have potential."

She released my arm and I felt a massive wave of confidence engulf me. Dr Rodriguez believed I had it in me to get the job done. Someone I'd never seen praise a soul or even be remotely nice to anyone or anything, thought that I had what it took to do this. Now I didn't have any room for failure. I had to succeed!

I walked back to my room and found Drew waiting there for me, sitting on the chair in the corner.

"So, you've got your first assignment now?" Drew asked, flipping her book closed and putting it down. "Where are you headed?"

"Yeah, I did, how did you know?"

"Every year it is the same day. I caught on quickly and remembered the date the second time around."

"Oh." I said. She had never mentioned how long she had been here before and this alluded to it being her third year here. "I haven't looked yet."

"Hand it over." Drew said, getting up and flopping down next to me. "I'll do it."

I handed it over to her and she looked at the piece of paper for a few seconds before looking up at me, a mild look of surprise on her face.

"You got Krasnoyarsk." She said simply.

"Where the hell is that? I've never heard of it. Ever." I said, bewildered by the name.

"It's in Russia." Drew said, "But don't worry, it isn't as cold as some other parts of Russia."

Thank God for that because I didn't know how I would have managed in such a terrible climate. I'd trained my mind and body in a warm environment and hadn't been outside or in freezing cold for a long time. The closest I'd got was how cold the rooms got.

"I know nothing about the place so you'll have to help me a lot." I said, nervously wiping my hands on my trousers. "That's what you're there for isn't it?"

"Of course," Drew said softly. "I'll always be there if you need me."

Drew had helped me out almost every day since I had come here and had protected me and taught me everything about this place that I needed to know. I was so grateful to have someone like her as my partner. Someone who was always looking out for me.

I leaned over to hug her and she instinctively wrapped her arms around me in return.

"What's this for?" She said, happier than before.

"I'm glad I have you as my friend." I said into her shirt.

Drew seemed quite touched by my words because she squeezed me tighter before letting go.

"I'll have your back, always." She said, the smile on her face showing she meant it.

"I'll do as much as I can for you too." I smiled back at her.

"Right, now back to business. We need to get you familiar with the territory, learn the basics of the language and learn about your target," She reached into her pocket and brought out a little calendar to check the dates. "And we only have twenty-eight days until you leave, so we've got to get all that done by then."

It seemed extraordinarily tedious and extremely hard, but if this was the time that they gave us then it obviously meant that they're confident in our abilities to get it done and I trusted them.

"Right, let's get started then." Drew said, standing up and rubbing her hands together. "We will get you ready for your first mission."

I twirled a pencil around between my fingers while the headphones on my head spewed the Russian that I was learning. I was able to understand Russian a lot better than I could read or write it, but Drew didn't seem worried about that.

I wrote down the answer to the question before taking my headphones off and handing the piece of paper back to Drew.

"Good, you've got it all down." She said, looking up at me and smiling. "I'm proud of you for getting this far; you've done amazingly well."

I swelled with pride from that compliment as I really cherished Drew's opinion.

"You're ready now," Drew suddenly said. "You may not believe me but you're ready for this and you're going to do great."

Today was my last day of training. The twenty-seven previous days had gone by in the blink of an eye and the next thing I knew, it was the day before I was travelling to Russia, specifically Krasnoyarsk, for my mission. I had studied the target; I knew my way around the whole city and I understood and could speak basic Russian. All in all, it had been a very productive month but I wasn't surprised that I had progressed so quickly with a teacher like Drew. She was someone who I knew cared for me and was willing to push me hard enough to get maximum effort.

"Thanks Drew," I said, feeling more relaxed than ever. "I feel a lot better about my chances because of all the training you got me to do."

"You've definitely followed it well. We may even be able to take the target down on the first try."

Taking down a target. That didn't seem so hard with all the experience Drew and I had combined. I felt excited at the prospect of completing a mission and showing everyone that I was capable.

Looking back on how I used to be made me anxious as I never wanted to be that vulnerable again. I was sure even the likes of Mamba would respect how far I'd come.

"Alright, get some sleep because tomorrow you're going to be setting off bright and early." Drew stood up and gave me a quick hug. "Make sure you get any last-minute practice in when you're on your way there as you won't have the time to do any training once you arrive.",

I nodded my head in acknowledgment before she walked out the door and shut it behind her.

Right. Sleep is what I needed, because for the past month I'd been staying up late memorising all the information and hadn't got much at all. As soon as my head hit the pillow I fell straight to sleep.

A banging on my door woke me up and I jumped straight up to open it.

"Get ready, you're leaving in ten." One of the trainers said, before walking off to the next room.

I quickly changed into clothes better fitting for a stealth mission before throwing all my necessities in a bag. More clothes, some weapons, and the map of the town I was going to be in, together with the Russian audio tapes, so I could learn more along the way. I left my room and walked down to the main hall and saw only a few other girls there. All of the others must have been leaving at different times.

"Line up!" Said the same woman who had been at my door. "We're leaving now. Go out to the cars and you'll get called into the specific one you're meant to travel in."

We all walked out together, them huddled together around each other, while I stayed off to one side not bothered by the situation.

We stood in a line and got called up one by one and each of us got in our separate vehicles.

There were no two girls in the same car, which was a smart idea as two girls would probably be able to take down the driver, even though they were highly trained.

"Put the blindfold on." The driver said, just as I had stepped into the car.

I tied it around my head and sat back ready to go.

The drive took a while and by the time we got to our destination I had lost track of how many different turns we had made or how far we had come.

"Take it off now." The driver commanded.

Removing the blind fold, I saw that we were at an airport. We were going to have to fly as Russia was across the water from where I was kept. I hadn't thought about the possibility that they had kept us in the same country as hadn't had time to spare any thoughts for it. Now, though, I had confirmation that we were.

We exited the car and I followed the driver into the airport like he had instructed me to.

I wasn't sure how we were going to get past security with my gear but I assumed that they had a plan for that so I wasn't worried at all.

"Where are we going?" I asked, as we were going in a different direction from all the other people flying out.

"Private plane." Was the short answer I got.

The assassin organisation must be extremely rich to be able to afford all this with no stress. A private plane, cars for all the girls and a massive underground base that was a few square miles at the very least. The resources it would take to build something like that would've been very hard to gather and then put together while also keeping the contractors who were building it in the dark. Whoever started this organisation was extremely dedicated to the cause.

We walked out of the building and onto the asphalt. The private plane was very close so it didn't take very long to get to it.

I was just about to ask who was flying when I saw the driver enter the cockpit and close the door behind him. I stood staring for a couple of seconds before walking to the back and sitting down in a seat. I was glad that I had brought all my preparation gear as it seemed I would have lots of time to study it all. No one else was on this flight. I had just put my headphones in and taken out the map of Krasnoyarsk when I felt the plane start to move. It didn't take much longer before we were shooting down the runway and taking flight. It wouldn't be long before we got to my destination so I needed to do as much as possible before we landed. I had to work my hardest because who knew what they would do to me and Drew if I failed this task.

I felt the plane shudder as it hit the ground. And we had landed. The flight hadn't taken as long as I thought but I was still able to get a decent amount of work done in that time. It took a few more minutes before we were at a complete stop and by that time, I had repacked my bag and was ready and waiting to go.

"I'm going to drive you to the place you're staying and then leave." The driver said, as he exited the plane with me in tow.

We went through the airport and into the parking lot outside where the car we were leaving on was parked. I got in and scanned the surrounding area as we drove along, hoping to memorise as much as possible if anything went wrong. Before I knew it, an hour had passed and we had arrived at the house I was staying at. It was a rundown little house out of the way and inconspicuous. No one would think to look here.

I got out of the car, taking my bag with me, and watched as my driver drove away. I wanted to get ready as fast as possible so I raced inside the house to unpack all my necessary gear.

The inside of the house was much better than the outside, although it still wasn't great. There was a lot of dust everywhere and it would appear that no one had lived in this house for years.

After putting my bag down, I walked around the house to get a better feel of it. Even though it was small I wanted to know every nook and cranny just in case. There was nothing much in the house except for a few shelves, drawers, a computer and a router for the WIFI. In the kitchen there was a little cooler that had some food and drink in it but it looked like I was going to have to get some more if I was to be here for more than a day or two, which was probably going to be the case. There were no bulbs, which I actually appreciated, as some light in a house that hadn't been used for a long time could draw suspicion and end up hindering me. I wasn't about to let the mission get ruined by something so simple.

I decided that since it was night time right now, this would be the best time to go out exploring the town and scouting out the house of my target.

I changed into all black clothes and made sure to put my daggers into the hidden sheaths in my trousers.

Having left the safe house I realised how dark it actually was and wished that I had something to help me see better in the night. There was nothing I could do though so I had to continue to try and get this over with as soon as possible. Since I had memorised the map of this town, I had no trouble traversing the area while staying out of sight at all times. I was being very cautious so it took double the time to complete the mile-long journey, compared to just walking there normally. In the end I didn't see anyone and no one saw me so it could be looked at as a waste of time, but I'd rather be safe than sorry.

I then arrived at the house - I shouldn't call it a house - it was a mansion.

Gated off from anyone else was the four-story mansion with massive windows either side of the double front doors. The garden outside was perfectly manicured and the house perfectly clean. The complete opposite from all the other houses surrounding it, including the rest of the city.

I knew my target was highly valued so they would definitely have security that would be triggered if I jumped over the gate. I needed another option.

Almost as if I had been heard, one of the staff members walked out, locking the gate electronically. She walked away in the opposite direction to me, thankfully oblivious to my presence. To be less conspicuous, I swiftly changed positions, moving silently towards her at speed. As I got up behind her, I snaked an arm around her neck and squeezed, making sure that I didn't do it too hard as I didn't want to kill her. Very quickly she was out cold. I took the badge, went over to the door, and swiped it. I knew I had to be quick because very soon, people would realise that I wasn't who I claimed to be. I didn't have time to switch uniforms or prepare one as I hadn't expected this opportunity this quickly.

The front door was already unlocked so I peeked round and as I saw no one, I stepped in.

The inside was as lavish as the outside or maybe even more. A massive golden chandelier was at the centre, with two spiral staircases on either side. Luckily, the floor was heavily carpeted, otherwise I would've had a really hard time keeping as quiet as possible.

Since there was no one around I decided to start my search from the bottom and make my way up. The door to the basement was in full view and it seemed less risky than going straight to the top, which was most likely more heavily guarded.

I silently opened the door and slipped down into the dim depths of the basement. The basement's sheer magnitude shocked me as I had expected it to be a relatively small place with one or two small side rooms, but this was huge and had enough rooms to be a house on its own.

I needed to check all of the doors to make sure everything was clear as I couldn't just burst right in. So, I put my ear to the first door and listened. After a few seconds I was sure the coast was clear so I noiselessly opened the door, peeked around it, and found a cell-like room with nothing but a metal table at the centre. The whole room was soaked with blood and reeked of death, so I quickly closed it and moved onto the next one. After seeing a few more rooms relatively in the same state, I heard something from the next door. There were screams so loud that it was as if they were next to me.

I cracked open the door to take a peek and was horrified at what I saw. Inside was a guy being tortured by two people in all black. The one on the right had a drill in his hand and the one on the left was currently using plyers to pull out the man's teeth. When I saw his face, my heart instantly dropped, and I almost collapsed.

It was Hugh!

Why was he here?

He shouldn't have been here!

This shouldn't be happening!

I froze, paralytic on fear, and thoughts started racing through my mind, muddling me up.

My hesitation was enough to let the other person line his drill up with Hugh's head and start drilling into his skull. Finally, his screams were enough to break me from my stupor and I rushed into the room, pulling my daggers out.

I shot an arm out towards the man holding the drill's neck with one of the blades and wrenched it back across, splitting open his throat.

I spun round to the other man but he was more prepared than his partner and was able to block my slash with his arm.

I felt pure hatred for these people and I needed to finish them off one way or another for having the audacity to do this to my friend.

I sized him up and noticed that his fighting stance was poor and he didn't seem to know how to handle the weapon that he was holding.

Taking advantage of this, I immediately stepped inside his guard, past his arm that was going for the kill and plunged my knife into the side of his throat, tearing it back out towards me.

Finally coming to me senses, I was breathing very heavily now and realised what I had done. But, unsurprisingly, I didn't hold any guilt or an ounce of sympathy for either of my victims.

"Hugh!" I cried, sprinting over to him and checking to see if he was okay. "Hugh...?"

I frantically felt the side of his neck for a pulse but there was nothing.

He was dead.

I dropped to the floor, suddenly weak and my spirit lifeless. Tears rolled down my cheeks and I clenched my shaking fists.

How could they kill Hugh and why was he even here? Did he get kidnapped like me or was it something different?

I knew that I would probably never get these questions answered as the two people who could be made willing were no longer on this earth.

Images of the two monsters laughing as they coolly murdered my friend flashed through my mind, reminding me of my failure to save him, specifically because I froze like a coward.

My phone vibrated in my pocket startling me and I scrambled to get it out before anyone could potentially hear it.

"Hello?" I said, not looking at the name on the screen before answering.

"Hey," Drew said, "Is something wrong?"

I had forgotten that I was getting help from Drew during this mission as the events that had just occurred were all I could focus on.

She must've noticed that I didn't sound myself at all.

"I went into th-the target's house...as I had a chance when I was just watching it and scouting it out. When I went inside...I decided to clear the floors from the bottom. And in the basement, there were a lot of different rooms, so I went into each one to make sure that no on-one was there..."

I paused and closed my eyes to try and stop the images of Hugh's dead body, that was right behind me, from flashing through my mind.

"What happened Katie?" She asked, cautiously.

"I found one of my friends from before I was kidnapped being tortured in one of the rooms," I said, letting out a quiet sob into my hands. "Because I was too weak to do anything about it, he was killed by them."

"I'm sorry." Drew said, her voice growing quieter. "You're still inside the house and need to get out qui-."

One glance behind me was all I needed to reject her notion - all the blood, the mess, the bodies strewn about across the room. I couldn't let it end like this. I had to get my revenge on everyone here.

"No!" I answered aggressively, suddenly determined. "I'm going to end it all here and now."

I didn't hear anything from the phone for a while and was getting worried that I wouldn't have any of Drew's help on this mission but then she spoke.

"Okay, I'll help you," She said. "But be careful. You don't want anything going wrong."

She started telling me everything that she was seeing outside. She had made sure that the alarm inside the house had been turned off for a few minutes so as to not alert the police whilst I was in the middle of the mission.

Memorising it all with haste, I hung up after she had finished and quietly crept upstairs onto the main floor, checking around corners to make sure that no one was there to surprise me. When I finished clearing the ground floor and established that no one was there, I knew that the target was upstairs and all the guards had to have followed. Since no one was on the main stairs or close to them I went up, thankful that they were also covered in carpet, making it very hard for anyone to hear me.

I reached the top of the stairs and checked each side, noting a guard with his back to me on my left and no one on my right.

Taking out all the guards would be my best bet as I didn't want anyone to be able to fight back or alert help on the outside.

Sneakily, I inched towards him, taking in the gun that was strapped over his shoulder. Looking at his clothes reminded me of the two people that tortured my friend, which quickly brought an uncontrollable rage to the surface, and I rapidly stabbed the guard in the side of the neck, slashing it across and cutting his throat open.

I felt a tingle of excitement as I watched his body drop to the floor, lifeless and bloody. A small smile grew on my face as I realised that I was capable of killing every last one of the people responsible for my friend's death and there was nothing that anyone in this house could do to stop me.

After the first guard, the others were a lot easier.

The joy I felt quickly grew.

I was having a tonne of fun killing all these lowlifes and watching the life drain from their eyes as they looked at me, with confusion, never to be answered.

They should already have known they were responsible for his death. All of them had paid for it with their lives so that they could no longer inflict pain upon anyone ever again.

There were quite a few guards leading up to my target's room but the numbers quickly grew as I reached the door to the bedroom.

It was time. This had to be done quietly but I didn't want hang about unnecessarily, so I had to go as swiftly as possible.

Springing out from behind my hiding spot, I savagely sliced the first guards throat, instantly turning to the side to slash at the other guard before he had a chance to react.

Slashing and stabbing were the only things on my mind as I decimated every human in my path. My half rage, half adrenaline state made the job much easier and I was much more efficient. With all the screaming and shouting that was going on I was very happy that every room in the house was sound proofed.

By the time I was finished, I was covered in blood, my disguise no longer a factor. Breathing savagely, I looked all around me, taking in all the bodies strewn across the floor. Looking at them all lying there made me feel a sense of pride at how good I had become. I had progressed even further than I had ever thought possible and I was overjoyed and excited.

I finally caught my breath and walked towards the door, making sure to keep an eye for any who could potentially ruin this mission when I was this close.

Subtlety wasn't something I wanted anymore so I barged into the room loudly and saw a man in white shirt and black trousers standing with his back to me.

"I told you not to come in here and disturb me," He shouted angrily. "So why are yo-"

His words fizzled out as he turned around and saw me covered in blood with a knife in my hand. I probably looked crazy right about now but that would only help here.

"Guards!" He yelled out, moving slightly back from me.

"No one can save you." I said coldly, walking up to his frozen frame and plunging the dagger right into his heart.

By the time he realised what had happened it was too late. Coughing up blood, he tried to remove the dagger but I drove it deeper in, twisting and turning it, as I did so.

"Die." I said, finally ripping the weapon out of him. I watched as he fell to the ground, unmoving, with glassy eyes.

He wasn't breathing anymore. He would never have anyone hurt again. He would never do anything again. Ever.

Finally, relief flooded through me as I re-sheathed my daggers and turned around to leave this forsaken place.

I ran out the room down the hallway, down the stairs and out the front door, making sure to utilise the cloth I had picked up before leaving to cover my face from any potential cameras.

I jumped over the gate and started running down the road into the dark, picking up on sirens in the distance.

The woman I stole these clothes from must've woken up and called the police. Because she worked for a person who was obviously rich, it was no surprise that the police would want to respond as quickly as possible.

But when they arrived, I wouldn't be there. There would also be no trace of me as the house had no cameras inside, I didn't use traceable clothes and I made sure to make it look more like a coordinated robbery gone wrong, instead of a murder, planned or otherwise.

I melted into darkness. The shadows kept me from being seen and I disappeared into the night, arriving at the safe house without anybody spotting me at all.

As soon as I got back, I called Drew on the secure line just to be safe.

"I did it," I said after she picked up. "On the first night too."

"Really?" She sounded genuinely surprised. "I didn't think that you were going to want to finish it tonight after what happened."

Maybe before, but now I was a different person and my responses to different situations weren't the same as they used to be. I'd now much rather get revenge than not do anything and avoid all conflict like I used to hope for.

"Yeah." I said. "It felt really good after what they did to Hugh."

"So, we will get a flight back for you tomorrow as they hadn't planned on you getting the job done this quickly, so I'll have to set things up for early tomorrow." The sound of a mechanical keyboard in the background meant that she was already working on it as we spoke.

"Okay, I'll call you back if anything goes wrong from now until tomorrow." I said.

"Make sure you do." Drew replied firmly. "I don't want anything to go wrong after so much has gone right."

"Bye Drew." I said smiling lightly.

"Bye." She said, sounding distracted.

Well then. I had to wait until tomorrow to do anything else. All I could do right now was make sure nothing suspicious was going on outside and no one found out I was here, which shouldn't be a problem considering I made sure I was never seen by anyone. That I was sure of.

Tomorrow I'd be back and training for the next mission. Hopefully, I would have Drew there as well. She wanted to come this time but rules are rules and at the Academy you cannot afford to break any rules.

CHAPTER 6

Walking down the hallways at night was always something I didn't like. The light was too dim, the air too damp and it was always a little bit too quiet.

That was, except for today.

Screaming could be heard where I was walking. It was faint, but clear as day. Screaming, silence. Screaming, silence. A constant cycle that carried itself through the air and sent an uneasy shiver down my spine. Nothing good was going on and I knew that going back to my room would be the best course of action, but my curiosity was getting the better of me and my legs just wouldn't stop moving forward towards the sound. I don't think I would have been able to stop myself even if I had tried.

"You should've thought of some method to make it harder for her than you did." A voice from in the room said, one that was all too familiar to me. "She showed how exceptional she is and since you've known her the longest you should have already accounted for that and made it harder accordingly. We can't get proper data out of this."

I heard more sounds from inside and finally decided to take a look and confirm my suspicions.

I was proved correct when Dr. Rodriguez came into view, although she was blocking my view of the person she was dealing with.

"The overall goal was a success, but not being able to gather enough data because she wasn't there long enough was something that you could've prevented."

They were talking about someone finishing a mission early and the only person who did was me. That meant that they were talking to and torturing someone close to me. In all my time here, I had never had a group of friends. I only had and shared anything with one person. That person was the only one I trusted. The only one that I cared about.

Drew.

Ana stepped aside and I could finally see that I was right.

It was Drew!

She was getting tortured by electric shock because they didn't have enough time to collect sufficient data on me. It was probably to do with my skill set in the field, something that couldn't really be tested here. Thinking about the reason why they wanted this information so much I concluded that this data would be used to determine who went on what missions and what kind of conditions they thrived in best.

It felt like something had shattered in my chest and I held my breath to stop the pieces flying out.

They were hurting my friend, my only friend, because of a small mishap they had made that could be easily fixed on the next mission, but apparently, they needed to hurt them so they'd understand. I suddenly felt much calmer than ever before. I knew what I needed to do now and I was going to succeed, even if I had to take everyone in this whole facility out to do it.

I needed to head back to my room and try to figure out a plan that could get me and Drew out of here safely. Although I really wanted to be out of here right now, I didn't have the time, resources or the opportunity. What I really hoped was that Drew would actually support me and trust me to get us out of here. Thinking about asking her to actually help me out wasn't something I wanted to do at all. It would again be my fault if anyone found out that she had tried to get out or helped me in my escape plan.

Before I knew it, I was back at my room, opening and then closing the door behind me. I didn't think that Drew would come over tonight so I didn't really have much to worry about as no one else came into my room, especially this late at night.

Thinking of ways to escape from this place was hard, mostly because I saw first-hand what they did to people who got caught. It was not pretty.

The biggest challenge would be to find the time to have a chance of escaping. We were under constant surveillance, which would limit me to the few minutes that we had alone when everyone went to lunch. A few minutes might be enough time for me to escape on my own, but with a second person it would take a lot longer. So doing it that way wasn't a viable option. Speaking to Drew might have given me some ideas but I wanted to come up with a solid concept first, before going to her about this, as actually having established the beginnings of a plan could get her on my side more easily. I needed to think more. I needed more time. Although, considering how fast like liked to send girls out on mission I wasn't sure I would get much.

Suddenly, I sat up, as if I had been stuck by lighting. I had just figured out how I was going to escape this place, together with Drew! It would be a struggle but I knew that together with Drew, I could accomplish anything. I had to do this and it had to work, because there were no other options. On my next mission, I would ask to bring along Drew and because they'd want her to be watching more closely, I was sure they'd agree to it. When we got to our destination, we would still complete the mission but take our time, and then when we'd finished, we would disappear and never turn up again, leaving the mission area and cutting all contact with anything to do with the Academy. For good.

Although I would have to think through the details more, I now had the basic structure of a plan and could tell Drew exactly what I was planning. I wanted to do it right now but it didn't feel right. I had to wait for her to come to me after the savage, brutal treatment she got because of me. I'd be more comfortable with that. I was sure she would be more open minded too if I waited because the fear they were instilling in her would have started to dissipate. I could only hope that this was the case anyway.

Whilst I wasn't happy that Drew was getting hurt, I was glad that her being uselessly abused had finally woken me from what felt like a daze that had plagued me since I started training here. I was now ready to do whatever it took to get us out of here and I wasn't going to stop trying until I had succeed.

I had now been assigned a new mission and to my surprise, and delight, Drew had been told that she was going along with me. I hadn't even had to ask. It was a real relief. They must have already been planning on sending her with me to try and slow down the mission compared to the 'failure' of last time.

Since the night I had seen Drew getting abused, she had been quieter, more reserved and didn't seem at all close to her normal self. She kept reminding me to take my time in the mission so I could get a better feel for how it was out in the field. That definitely couldn't have all been from the beating she got. I knew she was tough and wouldn't be that bothered by it because when comparing her personal safety and others, she'd always pick the other.

They must have said something about me - like how they were going to hurt me if I completed the mission too quickly, or something along those lines. Each time she brought it up I would make sure to reassure her that I would be fine and that if I ever went running off too far ahead in the mission, she'd always be there to stop me. This always seemed to give her more confidence and it came across like a sense of relief, which only further supported my theory.

Finding out when we would be leaving made me realise that I had to finally tell Drew that I was planning to escape on this mission. It was finally that time. Surprisingly, I didn't feel nervous at all. In fact, these days I didn't feel too much, apart from contempt towards the people running this torturous 'Academy', as they like to call it.

"Drew," I said slowly. "I have something to tell you."

"What is it?" she asked, distracted by the book she was reading.

"I'm planning on escaping here and I want you to come with me." I said it clearly but quietly. You never knew when people were around because everyone moved so silently.

Drew froze and looked up at me horrified. She glanced towards the door before quickly rushing over to me.

"Don't say those kinds of things," She hissed at me, putting a hand over my mouth. "You do know what kind of trouble you would get into if anyone heard you, right?"

I slowly nodded and then gently pried her hand off my face, giving her a serious look.

"I know what they can do, and I know what they are capable of," I said confidently, "And that is the exact reason why I want to leave this god forsaken place and go anywhere else!"

She stared at me wide eyed, not believing what was coming out of my mouth and how I could have so much confidence. I didn't really understand it either but it was a sudden transformation that started, firstly after my first mission, and was completed after I saw what they did to Drew.

"I've got a lot of it pla-"

"No," Drew said flatly. "No way in hell am I going to allow the only person that I know in here to get hurt, or even killed."

"Listen!" I said, grabbing her by the wrists. "I've been planning this for a few weeks, since I came back from my first mission actually, and I've had a lot of time to decide whether I can really pull this off or not and I've come to the conclusion that yes, I can do it. I could do it alone but I know that I'll be much happier and it'll be a lot easier to do together with you."

We sat there staring at each other, neither wanting to be the first one to move. The spell was broken when the sound of the alarm when off, reminding everyone that it was time for lunch.

"We will talk about this afterwards, okay?" I said, making her look at me.

"Okay." She said, seemingly resigned for the talk later that day.

Lunch was as uneventful as always. After the first few weeks and the first few examples of what happened if they didn't sit quietly and eat, no one tried anything anymore. They all just sat quietly until it was time to go back to their rooms.

I thought that I might have sympathy for leaving these people behind but I really didn't care as none of them meant anything to me and I didn't personally know any of them.

They all left me alone and never interacted with me either. Well, the nice ones at least did.

People were very hostile to me at lunch time and in the hallways but they never did anything physical. Which is lucky for them because the punishment they'd get for damaging one of their fellow associates would be severe and ruthless.

By the time Drew and I got back to my room I had a clear train of thought on what I wanted to say to her to get her to come with me and escape together.

But before I could start, she turned to me and said four words that made me stumble back in shock.

"I'll come with you."

My argument died before it left my mouth. I didn't even have to plead my case like I thought I was going to have to. In fact, I didn't even end up having to do any sort of convincing.

"Really?" I asked, still very astounded yet curious. "What made you change your mind?"

"I've had enough of it here. Constantly worrying over whether or not you're going to be hurt, if I'm going to be taken out so I can't protect you?" She looked determined now. "If you decide to escape in the future without me anyway, I would never be able to be there for you again."

I reached for her and gave her a hug.

"Thank you."

She hugged me back and then we both pulled away. It looked like it was now business time.

"We're only going to have one shot at this because the security they'll put up after this will stop anyone escaping from here ever again. So, the plan has to be perfect." Drew said.

"We've got an amazing opportunity on our next mission," I added, "Is there any sort of tracker that they put on us while we were away?"

"No, they trust that they've beaten all the fight out of the older ones, the ones who have been here longer." As she mentioned this it looked like she was getting more and more confident, convincing herself that we could pull this off. "They let us control the missions fully and do what we please but we're going to have to find some way to stay off the radar. Go someplace that they would never think to look for us."

"I know a place." It had suddenly clicked. A place that they wouldn't check. The last place that they'd assume I would go to. Where it all began. "My home."

"Come on, quicker!" Drew said, holding the punching bag to make sure it didn't stray too far away from me.

My breath came out in urgent pants as I punched quicker and harder, trying to squeeze out every last drop of effort before the minute was up.

"And time!" She said, moving away from the bag and throwing me a bottle of water. "Well done, you've already improved so much in the last few weeks."

Although we knew that we were going to be leaving soon and all of this fighting and stamina training might mean nothing considering the little time we had to train. We were still going to take all the precautions possible and try and get as close to our physical peak before leaving. We didn't want to leave anything to chance as next week was going to be one of the most crucial weeks in our lives. It was going to be a struggle to get back to my home, but that didn't mean that it was impossible as there was always a way.

"Have you got any idea how we are going to reach your home town from the mission area?" Drew had asked when I mentioned going back to my house.

Although I didn't have a definite idea on how it was going to go, one of the main options that I was considering was travelling by boat. We could hide on a ship that was going to the United Kingdom with food and water that we would pack, sneaking off afterwards before anyone noticed us.

It wasn't much of a well-thought-out plan but it was all I could come up with in such a short space of time. I was sure more ideas would come to me after we arrived at our mission home base because we would get to scout out the actual area, which was always better than on a screen. I would also now have Drew coming up with plans as well which would make the process twice as efficient. Now, all we could do was try our hardest and hope that everything went according to plan. Otherwise, we would be in real trouble.

It was finally the day we were scheduled to leave. We had packed everything that we needed – weapons, clothes and electronic devices - so that we could communicate with the people back here. The other things that we would need for our escape plan would be bought at our destination as too many questions would be asked if we took food and water or other things in that vein when we could get them there. Simple was better, especially in situations like this.

"You made sure that you have everything?" Drew asked, checking her bag one last time.

"Yep," I said, "I've made sure to tick everything off my list."

"Good," Drew said, before muttering under her breath "This is my final chance."

"I know," I said softly, trying to comfort her.

I didn't have to mentally prepare myself for things of this nature as I was so confident in my own, and Drew's ability, leaving no room for doubt in my mind that we weren't going to succeed in our escape attempt.

"Let's go then." I said, slinging my bag over my shoulder and walking out the door.

"Right behind you." Drew said, grabbing her bag and catching up to me.

Walking down this hallway had felt different ever since that night I had decided I was going to get out, but today, it felt even more different from any other time before. I felt sad in a way, like I was leaving something important behind and although being in this place had made me a person that I was prouder of, it was in spite of this facility and the people inside, not because. I wouldn't have wished anyone to go through what I'd been through here but it didn't make the fond feelings and memories that I'd developed go away any faster.

Before I knew it, we were on our flight, flying out to our destination. As I watched the ground slowly change from land to water, I felt a sense of relief. We had past the first stage without any complications.

Now, it was up to us to complete the next stages and get away from this organisation. Compared to the time I'd spent away, it would only take a little bit of time to get back to my town.

To pass the time, I asked one of the questions that I'd always wanted to ask Drew: what her family life like was before we got to this place. I had never had the courage before but now that we had left that place and those people, the adrenaline was making me feel more confident in my decisions.

"Hey, Drew?" I asked, glancing to my right where she sat. "What was your life like before you came to this place?"

She was quiet for a long time, almost to the point where I didn't think that she would answer. I had looked away, feeling deflated, before I heard her start to speak.

"I moved around a lot when I was a kid because it was only me and my mum and she had to take whatever work she could get." Drew had a faraway look on her face as she said this, like she was reminiscing. "Although we had a happy life and were really close, I had always felt that something was wrong. She told me that us moving around was all for her work but in reality, the assassination organisation wanted me and had tried to take me, meaning that every few months we would move to try and escape them."

She slowed down for a bit but I was prepared to wait until she was ready to tell me the next part. It wasn't until a few minutes later that she actually continued though.

"One morning when I was supposed to be going off to school, I came downstairs to find my mum covered in blood and two people wearing black standing over her. As soon as they noticed me, they lunged and before I knew it, I was in that wretched place." By the end of the story Drew had become quieter and didn't look like she was going to talk again, lost in her own thoughts.

Now I had learnt what had transpired, it made my ember of rage towards the Academy grow exponentially for hurting Drew's mum and for trying so cruelly to get her. While I didn't have to deal with them hurting my family physically as well as emotionally, this was something that she had to deal with. I needed to help Drew, at all costs, regain her family and take down the organisation. This was a situation that made me feel as if my experiences were diminished. While Drew had been constantly worrying about her mother's health, I had complained to her about matters that now seemed trivial. A fire was lit under me. I was going to do whatever it took to reunite my friend with her mother. No matter what it was that I had to do, I was prepared.

We arrived at the house and once the driver was long gone the first thing we did was leave our bags and go into town to scout out the immediate area. We were in a town in Paris off the north coast. It was the closest we could get to going back to where I lived without actually landing in England. The city of Calais. Before we had come here, we had researched the closest point where boats came and went to the UK. Luckily enough, there was a ferry that ran from Calais to England that was only a mile or two away from home base. This would make travelling to and fro much easier than we first thought.

Things so far were going well, but if the next part of the plan didn't go exactly how we wanted it to, then nothing else we did afterwards would be of any use.

"Looks like everything is the same as we saw it on the map." Drew said, as we walked along.

"Luckily," I said. "It would've been a pain if it had been all different."

"I'm just glad that this means we can leave at the earliest possible moment."

"Me too." I smiled over at Drew as we continued deeper into the town.

There were a lot of narrow roads all around which would really help conceal us at night as we would be very hard to spot.

Unfortunately, something we had seen earlier was correct. The area around the dock was cordoned off with wired fencing. To add to that, it was an open space, an open area where we would easily be spotted if we weren't careful.

"Damn," I said, "This adds a bit more preparation work for us."

"I wouldn't want it to be too easy," Drew said, smiling over at me. "Otherwise you would know for sure that something was going to go wrong."

"Fair enough." I said, laughing.

Now that we had done our main exploration of the area, we needed to go back and get everything ready. Something to act as a cushion for the spiky wire at the top of the fence was needed. We already had dark clothes for the mission and we needed to wait at least one night to scout the area in darkness as well, to observe how many people would be around or if it would be empty.

Once all that was done, and if everything looked fine, only then would we be able to leave on one of the ferries.

When we got back and because we had time to kill, Drew suggested going out and trying some of the local food. I hadn't had anything other than the food they served at the Academy but it had got worse and worse since I arrived there. Probably a side effect of them redesigning it to still carry the nutrients needed but exclude any of the other unnecessary parts. Strolling around the area we decided on a restaurant called Le Grand Bleu. It seemed to have nice looking food and I was hungry so didn't have any objections.

When we went in, we got seated and then ordered. We hadn't been sitting there for long when I saw two people walk in, the uniforms they were wearing indicating that they worked on the docks. I glanced at Drew and knew that she had seen them as well. It was our lucky day because when they were seated, which happened to be near us, they started talking about their job and some of the information that was very useful. They mentioned how quiet it usually was, especially at night when the ferries would leave. Not thinking or caring anyone would be listening to them, they also mentioned one of the entrances that staff entered from. They were happy that no one checked it because it allowed them to sneak out when they were supposed to be working.

Our luck was amazing. We had impulsively gone to this restaurant at a weird time, not expecting anything to happen and ended up encountering two people who worked at the very place we were trying to sneak into. They had talked completely openly about their jobs the whole time.

We finished eating because the food was good but left quickly afterwards to prepare for the inevitable escape attempt later. Our plans had changed but our goal remained the same as it always was.

Before we knew it, it was dark. We had everything we needed and quickly left the house, going in the direction of the entrance we had scouted out earlier. After sneaking through the town - we didn't want to draw any attention to ourselves as outsiders - we came to the barbed wire fence which was quickly covered and scaled. We didn't see many people around but we still had to be careful.

While sneaking through the dark, I suddenly heard footsteps close by, causing me to duck behind a crate. The person was very close and kept getting closer. I really hoped that they weren't going to get any nearer but regrettably, he did. He saw me. Quick as a flash I drew my dagger, slashing at his throat before he could yell. He stumbled a bit before collapsing, me catching him in my arms. Drew, who had been too far away to help with this, came over to me and helped push the body off the side of the dock into the water, washing away any evidence that we had been here. Surprisingly, I didn't feel anything after that kill. I didn't feel panicked that I had done something wrong. In fact, it felt like I had just completed an everyday task.

Once we got through that ordeal, the rest of the trip was uneventful and we got onto the ferry without any more casualties. We decided to enter a small closet that was tucked away behind some barrels and stayed there for the night so that we had the smallest chance possible of being spotted. The jet lag, combined with the fact that it was late suddenly hit me and I felt quite tired.

"I'll take the first watch and wake you up in four hours." Drew said, setting up by the door.

"Thank you." I said, lying down on the cold hard floor.

It wasn't pretty but beggars couldn't be choosers and soon, I was dozing off into the depths of sleep.

Our journey was uneventful and we successfully snuck off the ferry without being spotted. The hard part now was going to be staying off the radar while travelling to London. Where I lived. We didn't have a car or any identification so our only real options were train tickets, walking or travelling by different buses. Since it seemed easiest, we decided on going by train. It would take a few hours and quite a lot of changes but we needed to be discreet. The best way to do that was to try and stay in crowed areas, away from main roads and streets, making it harder to spot us.

"You got the tickets?" I asked Drew, as I had been acting as a lookout.

"Got them," She said, flashing them to me before handing one over. "Let's go."

I didn't let my thoughts drift too much, otherwise the anxiousness would probably appear on my face. I didn't want to be the reason this failed, especially since it was going so well. Although the train journey was long, because I was so focused on the fact that I was going home, it didn't seem like a long time. It was only when we got off the train that I was finally hit with the reality that I was going to see my family and friends again.

How much had they changed? I wondered. I knew I had changed a heck of a lot since the last time they had seen me and what if they didn't like the person I'd become? I cared less about people's lives and had no problem killing. My personality had become a lot more rigid and I was sure that I was a lot more observant to compensate for how jittery I got. Just as I was about to go spiralling down that line of thought Drew stopped me.

"I know you're worried about what is going to happen when we get there," She said, facing me, "But worrying won't solve anything. All you can do is your best and if they still don't accept you then it's their loss."

What Drew was saying made complete sense but it didn't make it any easier to digest.

"I know." I said, swallowing visibly.

"I'll always be here for you." Drew said it as if it was the most normal thing in the world.

"Thank you."

I wasn't sure if she even realised how much that had meant to me but I was eternally grateful for the love and care she had for me, how much she did for me without complaint and how she was willing to blindly trust me. I was not sure that I could've found a better person and friend in such a hell hole.

As we walked through town, I was noticing all the little things that I so carelessly over-looked before as everyday occurrences. The kids having fun in the playground, the school kids walking back from school talking to each other and having a laugh. People sitting on one of the benches, on their phones, looking to have a great time. Despite everything that was bad about this place I had missed it when I was gone. The feel of the town that you grew up in wasn't something that you could easily replace. All of my experiences in this area were coming back to me. Things that I hadn't thought of in years. Although we were back in my home town, I didn't want to go home straight away. I wanted to make sure that nothing was going to happen to my family if we were to show up. The only way to do that was to wait a bit and make sure that nothing would go wrong.

As if my thoughts had manifested, I suddenly felt eyes on me. Glancing towards Drew I saw her looking back at me, confirming my suspicions.

Had they found us already? No, it couldn't be that. The only answer I could think of was that they had someone stationed here from the beginning. Maybe even from before they kidnapped me. Now fully focused on my surroundings, I took Drew to the closest hotel, keeping an eye out in case the person decided to be more obvious in their stalking.

We reached the hotel without spotting anything suspicious but I knew for a fact that someone had been following us. I just had to hope that they couldn't get into contact with Ana in the next few days otherwise we would be royally screwed.

We paid for the room with cash using fake names and then went up to our room.

"So, we had someone following us." Drew said, a deadpan expression on her face.

"Yeah," I said, flopping onto the bed. "I think that they are going to try and get into here later tonight, especially since they now know exactly where we are staying."

Drew took a second to think before smirking over at me.

"You purposefully led them here so that when they try and break in to do whatever they want to us, we can instead ambush them and capture them?"

"Exactly!" I said. "And I don't think that they're going to contact anyone about this either."

I didn't know why but my gut was telling me that this person wasn't going to contact anyone unless things started going extremely wrong.

"We should get to work then." Drew said, getting out the stuff we had available for the makeshift security for our room.

"Let's do it." I said, grabbing the wiring out of the bag.

A few hours later we had set everything up and were waiting for the person to try and come in. Because we knew that it was someone from the Academy, we had to improvise our traps so that they wouldn't be nullified straight away. Luckily, we didn't have to wait long for the person to start their attempt. All the lights were off and since we had nothing to help us see in the dark, all we could use was the limited moonlight allowed through the curtains.

The lock was being jiggled around and it wasn't long before it clicked and the door slowly moved to an open position. The person was obviously being extremely careful as they knew who we were. As soon as the door opened halfway, our first trap triggered and the wire made a stack of bottles fall over onto the person, in an attempt to startle them more than anything.

Drew and I quickly rushed up to the door but by the time we got there the person was already sprinting down the pitch-black hallway. Going out of the hotel would void our advantage of already knowing the place inside out. Quickly realising that the only exit was just below our window, I hurried over to it. All I saw before the person vanished around a corner into an alleyway was a flash of red hair fading into the night.

We had decided that while we still had the chance, we would go to my family house to see my mum. It may be dangerous but the more I thought about it the more I got reassured by the fact that Ana hadn't had anything done to her so far.

She had talked about mentality. Breaking someone to a point. But I thought that even she realised that killing someone's parent was something that you should try and avoid as it would completely and utterly fuck up someone mentally, well past the point that she was aiming for. It would destroy them.

When I glanced over at Drew, who was stacking the bottles up again in the same place, my mind instantly went back to the person who tried to break into our place.

We didn't have much on them but what really helped to narrow down our candidates when looking at our suspects was that the person was a woman with red hair. Nothing else but that was known, and we had to deal with it. Lack of information on a target was something we were taught and trained to be able to deal with back at the Academy. We both felt that we had learned a lot from that and were ready to begin our search when we left to go meet my mum for the first time in a long time.

Now that I didn't have much space for thoughts about nervousness, I actually felt excited. I was getting to see my mum again, my best friend too. The ones who had always been there for me. I just hoped that in my time here I would get to see everyone else before anything more happened - Jessica and Jill, now that Hugh was no longer with us. Those three people were all I had left from my past life I was looking forward to seeing. After being gone for that long, in such a horrible place, I didn't feel the need or desire to see Blake. He didn't matter as much to me as before. In fact, he didn't matter to me at all anymore. All the feelings that I had

had for him had dissipated and vanished, never to be seen again.

Suddenly, I didn't feel nervous anymore and I knew exactly why. Even with my thoughts drifting back to all the horrible possibilities that could happen, I didn't let it take away from the simple fact that I had only just realised. I now had the power to protect my family and friends. I wasn't weak anymore. I had trained for months, and now I had better control of my emotions. My fighting ability was also nowhere near where it had been even a few months ago. My progression was exponential and the main reason for that was the last reason that I wasn't scared anymore; Drew.

I now had an ally at my side, ready to help and defend all the people I cared about, because she felt the same way about me. I had lost a lot over the months I was gone, but that only changed me and, because of the support that I'd had, it was for the better. No longer did I have to fear losing my family or friends. No longer did I have to fear for my own safety. No longer did I have to do everything alone. I had someone to help me out and I was getting to see my friends and family again. There was not much more I would've wished for if I could.

It was time now. We had arrived outside my house. It was exactly how I remembered it. The small garden surrounding the pathway that was littered with cracks; flowers falling onto it making it seem even smaller, one of the front windows always half open, letting a cool breeze waft through the house. As I looked up, I noticed that even my bedroom hadn't changed in all this time. I guess my mum still had hope after all.

"Let me do this alone to begin with." I knew that it would be easier with Drew, but I wanted to see my mum face to face alone for the first time. Without anyone else there.

Drew nodded at me and backed off a little way down the road, making sure that she was still within a certain distance so that she would be able to come if need be.

I walked up to the door and hesitated, my hand on the door knocker. My mum's car was here so I knew that she was still home and hadn't gone out. Finally overcoming my fears, I struck the door twice with the knocker.

It took a few beats before I heard any movement from inside.

"Coming!" I heard my mother's voice yell out kindly as I saw her moving through the obscured glass window. "How ca-"

Her voice cut out as she gazed at my face. Her eyes became misty before I decided to break the silence.

"Hey mum..." I said awkwardly, not knowing what else to say.

"Katie...? Katie is that you?" Mum said, the shock clearly still taking affect.

"Yeah mum, it's me."

She broke down sobbing as she flung her arms around me, dragging me towards her. As she did, I could feel all the tention in her body start to disappear into nothingness. Although I wasn't able to show too much emotion externally, internally I was overjoyed. It felt like a piece of me that I had lost had finally come back to me. After all this time I finally got to see my mum again and she was okay. No one had hurt her or done anything of the sort. I knew that later there would be a lot of questions but, right now, I just wanted to stand here and enjoy the moment. A moment I had been craving since I was taken, and now, I finally had it.

After mum had finally stopped crying and we had let go of each other, I invited Drew back to the house. Mum took an instant liking to Drew, liking the fact that she had been the one helping me on my journey back. I didn't even have to tell her. Mother's intuition, I guess.

Now that our reunion was mostly over, I knew that I would have to explain everything to her, but I had told her that I wanted to tell Jessica and Jill at the same time and so she had gone to call them.

I was aware that she suspected that something wasn't quite right because she frowned when I didn't use Hugh's name as well, obviously not suspecting or expecting that I was at the scene of where it all happened.

I'd seen a lot of movies where the main character kept a big secret from the others to 'keep them safe' but I'd always hated it when they did that. Not telling them would put them more at risk, compared to them knowing the full situation and the risks out there. Before I was taken, everyone trusted me. Everyone knew that I wasn't a rash person who did something for no reason and if they still thought of me in that way, then it was going to be even easier.

Outside, I heard Jessica's car pull up fast. Two doors opened and closed very quickly and loudly before they knocked on the door, seeming to slow down on their approach.

When the door was opened for them by mum, they burst through, looking around frantically before their eyes fell onto me.

"Katie!" Jessica said, rushing up to me with tears in her eyes. She flung her arms around me and pressed her face into my shoulder.

I felt another pair of arms coming around from my side and realised it was Jill. Both my friends were with me again. Stretching to reach them both, I wrapped my arms around them. I started chuckling at how squished I was in-between them, which got them to notice how much they were squashing me, causing them to be a little laxer in their grip. They pulled back and just stared at me for the longest while and I did the same with them. It felt like I hadn't seen them in a lifetime, and for me, that was somewhat true. I was a completely different person now. Although I had still retained some of the traits I had before, a lot of them had gone away and new ones had arisen. New and better traits because I was a better person now.

"You've been gone for such a long time." Jill said. She stopped to collect her thoughts before continuing. "What happened?"

"And who is that?" Jessica asked, noticing Drew behind me.

Drew had stayed out of all the commotion but when she heard that, she answered.

"I'm Drew. Katie's friend." She said, replying to Jessica's question straight away. "And as for what happened...actually, I think it would be better if Katie were to tell you."

And so, I did. I told them the whole story and they stayed quiet throughout. I thought they might have wanted to ask questions while I told them what had happened to me over that time, but they just stared at me wide eyed. Obviously shocked.

"...and so, after we got off the boat we came back here."

I waited for someone to speak up but it took quite a while before I saw my mum open her mouth to say something.

"You went through all that?" Her eyes scanned me as she said that, checking for anything physically wrong with me.

I looked over to Jessica and Jill to gauge their reaction and they seemed as shocked as mum, or even more so.

Just before anyone could ask any more questions I felt as if something was wrong. Looking over to Drew I saw the same expression on her face, confirming my fears. Realising that I was acting weird, they all looked at me but I put my finger to my lips, letting them know to be quiet. Everything just felt wrong.

I closed my eyes and listened carefully. At first, I could only hear the sound of my heartbeat, but after a few seconds I heard distinct the sound of someone softly stepping on leaves right outside the window. That person who broke into mine and Drew's room must have contacted the Academy and they had sent someone more skilled to try and either get us to come back, or get rid of us if we didn't cooperate.

Knowing that alerting the person to the fact that we were onto them was a bad idea, I didn't move towards the sounds, but instead stayed exactly where I was. I needed to figure out where this person would come from and the best way to do that would be to put myself in their shoes.

The front door? That option is off the table straight away; it's too conspicuous. Back door? They would have to climb over the fence, which would make a lot of noise as it was old. The best way to get into the house would be through one of the windows. Since the back garden was off limits, that meant that they would try and sneak through one on the front or one on the side. We had two windows around the side of the house but was too small and the other one had bars on the inside, which would be too noisy and would take too long to cut through. So, the only window left that they could come from was my room window, which was at the front of the house.

I pulled my daggers out, causing mum, Jessica, and Jill to flinch, and pointed towards the ceiling to Drew. Since she hadn't had the time to do a full scouting of the house, she wouldn't have been able to come to the conclusion that I had come to.

Nodding, she pulled out her own weapon.

Hearing my window quietly open with the small squeak as always, I was proven right. Unfortunately, at that exact moment I heard someone climbing over the back-garden fence.

Two people? I guess that makes sense since both me and Drew were here. I didn't know why I hadn't thought of that sooner.

Drew was already quietly moving towards the back door, having decided that she would deal with the person outside and I was left with the one upstairs.

"You already know I'm here, don't you Katie?"

That voice. I recognised it. I couldn't place from where but I knew the person's voice.

Knowing that there were only two people around, I encouraged Mum, Jessica, and Jill to find somewhere safe in the house to hide, sticking together. Drew could take care of things on her end. It was only dependant on whether I could on mine.

I heard someone walking down the stairs, but it wasn't until they reached halfway that I was actually able to see their feet. A sword in hand, she leisurely continued down the stairs until I could see her whole being. A red mane flowed behind her as she slowly reached the bottom and only then did I recognise her. Blake's sister, Matilda, stood in front of me!

"It's been a long time, hasn't it?" She said with a sadistic smile.

"What?" I said, utterly confused that she was one of the people after me.

"Is that how you greet old friends?" She said, laughing maniacally. "You do know that I am the reason that you were able to enter the Academy in the first place, right?"

She was the reason that I was taken! Which meant that she had been planning this all along. When I had slept over at her house. When she had driven me home. That strange feeling I got back then in the car must have been my intuition knowing that something was wrong with her. Unfortunately, at that time, I had no experience with any sort of danger so didn't realise what that feeling was. Afterwards, I had too much going on to think about a moment that was, at the time, trivial to me.

"So, you're the reason for all of this." I said. My confusion dissipated and I suddenly didn't really care about what she had to say anymore.

"After all my hard work of bringing you in and this is how you repay me." She laughed maniacally again.

"I'm going to kill you." I said, in a cold tone that wiped all the joy from her face.

"I'd like to see you try." She said, before suddenly lunging at me with her sword. I deflected it with one of my daggers and aimed the other one at her heart but she quickly jumped back out of the way.

"This is going to be more fun than I thought." She said wickedly, before increasing her speed, letting me know that the first strike was only a warning. The calm before the storm.

She was correct about that. Blows came from either side trying to gain dominance but not being able to break through each other's defences. It wasn't until she surprised me with a kick that it started to change. I quickly recovered and went at her again, this time using her own style, but faking out at the last possible moment so that I could go in with my daggers again.

Soon we were consistently skimming blows off each other, neither getting any clean hits apart from her kick and the first time I had faked a punch. We matched each other too well.

But, unfortunately for her, I had studied the techniques on how to be more effective just before we came back here and one of the things Drew showed me was how to constantly change up the patterns of attack to make it that much harder for your opponent to read. She seemed surprised and angered by my constant change in attack and didn't look so cocky anymore.

Just as I was getting her into a corner, I felt a sudden pain in my arm. Because I had become distracted, I missed the small knife that she had taken out with her other hand and thrown into my arm. Although the pain wasn't too bad, my grip was slowly fading and I knew that I would have to fight with only one dagger soon, which wasn't very convenient, especially against the longer reach that she had with her sword. Faltering for a split second, Matilda pounced on me like a lion to a wounded gazelle.

Luckily for me, I was much more capable than that. Acting on instinct, I jumped back, just getting out of range for her first swing, leaned back for her second and ducked under and forward while scrapping one of my daggers across her leg. Her knee skimmed my ribs as she kept up her assault, but I dodged the majority of the blows. Her barrage carried on but I had an answer to all her questions. She couldn't get a big hit on me. She had lost her knife and the advantage of a surprise attack which she first had when she started her onslaught.

"Is that all you've got?" I questioned, realising that I was actually much better at this than a few weeks before. The training sessions with Drew really had helped.

I wasn't even going at my maximum and I was able to keep up with her rage induced best. Before this, I hadn't had much of a chance to test out my new skills, but now that I was finally getting to, I was really happy.

While defending myself from her vicious charge, I made sure to keep an eye on the surroundings to make sure that everything was alright with Drew and that no one else had decided to join in.

As I did so, I saw mum, Jessica and Jill hurriedly trying to move to a safer location as we had backed up near them. Matilda also saw that and that was when she decided to make her move. Changing up her style she fumbled with her sword before continuing her pace. The mistake that she made with her sword threw me off and I wasn't prepared for the next blow that came and thus was knocked to the ground. Matilda ran towards them, obviously trying to cut them down, but as I still had my daggers in my hands, I wasn't worried. Before even getting into a seated position I threw one of them at her back. She crumpled to the floor as it had hit something vital. Getting up slowly, I walked over to her and lowered myself to her level.

"I need to protect my family; I need to protect my family..." She mumbled the same thing over and over again, not looking like she was in the same world as the rest of us.

So even she had stuff she wanted to protect. This insane person had a family and friends - people that she cared about and wanted to keep safe. Even with all that, she went after mine, intent on destroying them as best she could. I guess I could relate. Before anyone could react, I pressed the knife up against her throat and harshly dragged it across. Although I had a family and friends that I wanted to protect and I knew that she did too, my family and friends were the only ones that mattered to me. I didn't care what happened to the people that this psycho treasured.

Dashing outside, I saw Drew just finishing the fight. Whoever it was that she was fighting was suddenly headless and then their body dropped to the floor.

Before I arrived by her side she spoke up.

"That was Mamba."

The person who had tortured me and put me through so much when I had first arrived at the Academy. The one who had plagued my nightmares had been slain and was no longer on this earth. The satisfactory feeling that coursed through me was pure joy. I didn't fear her anymore but that didn't mean that the torment, while I was weak, didn't have any effect on me. I looked across at Drew and she realised that I had something planned.

"I want us to go back." I said.

She looked at me surprised, but understood I had more to say and let me carry on.

"They aren't going to stop coming after all the people I cared about. The only way for us to stop something happening again would be if we went back there and destroyed it from the inside."

I had told my mum and friends what Drew and I planned to do. I could see the conflicted look in my mother's eyes, especially seeing first-hand how easily I was able to end a life in such a brutal fashion. The look in her eyes was all I needed to see to hesitate on my decision to go back but, after she realised how much I needed to do this and that I was doing it for her and the people I cared about, her eyes became much less sad and she looked proud. Proud of how much I cared about everyone still and how far I would go for them. I thought that she would've protested much more, but it seemed that she already knew, to some degree, that I was going to want to go back to end this once and for all. That's mums, I guess. They really did know everything. I knew that she wasn't afraid of me and still wholeheartedly trusted me, and knowing that helped my decision feel more real.

My friends were of course very sad. I had just come back. But after I explained how they wouldn't be safe with the Academy still around they understood. They didn't like it and I could tell that Jessica wanted to come along with me but felt like she would be a burden.

She would be, unfortunately, but that didn't mean I would miss her any less, or that my want for her to come with us would wane even a little.

Only Drew and I had the ability, practise, and knowledge to be able to defeat such a formidable enemy. So, we had to try with everything we had and not let anything or anyone get in our way. If something like that happened, we wouldn't be able to protect them. I could not allow anyone to be in danger anymore. It was then that we decided to spend the day together. I didn't know if I was going to see my family or friends again because if we failed, then we'd both be dead. We spent the day out with everyone trying to have fun and doing things that I had missed while kidnapped.

Although the thought of how we were going to get our objective done was hanging over me, I still enjoyed the day. The distraction really helped me relax, which in turn helped with the planning that was going on in my mind. Since it was decided that Drew and I would go back to help destroy that vile place, I had been formulating some plans in my head of how we were going to do this. I had been struggling with it up until spending time with everyone. I hadn't been excited about it because I was focused on other things, but I guess I needed to take a step back and calm myself to be able to see the full picture.

I hadn't come up with a full plan but I was much further along compared to before. The probability of us getting through this relied heavily on the plan that both me and Drew were able to come up with. I had come up with a lot of different ways we could avoid suspicion on the way there but I was still lacking on how we were supposed to get into that place. The saving grace was that because I had gone on two missions, I had seen where the lair was and was able to more accurately picture the layout in my mind. Drew had obviously seen the place before but being able to picture it in your own head is a massive advantage in any situation.

I looked over to Drew and saw that while she looked completely focused on planning, her mind was drifting. Worry was evident on her face.

"I know we can do this." I said, walking over to her.

She looked up, interrupted from her uneasy thoughts.

"I know it sounds like a suicide mission, but," Adding emphasis at the end, I continued. "It's us that are doing this."

I wasn't saying this to be conceited, or frame us as the best in the business, but the trust between us was enough to rival anyone at that place. Our goals and passion to take down these people was enough to carry us over the edge to being as optimised as we could at this very moment. It was not like we had no chance of struggling tremendously and failing. Unfortunately for them, we were together and could rely on each other wholeheartedly. The girls that they had now lacked the one thing that we had built up and kept throughout the whole ordeal: Being able to trust someone with our lives.

It wasn't something that any of the girls in either mine or Drew's years had kept hold of after all the hardships they had been through. Not one of them had been able to stave off the mentally debilitating fear that was instilled every day. They lost this piece of themselves because they didn't have someone to help keep them from going over the edge. No one was strong enough to do that before Drew and that would be their downfall. No one knew the type of relationship that me and Drew had. They didn't realise that we actually cared for each other and would put our lives on the line for the other.

This gave us a massive advantage in surprise. Not only did they have to deal with two people who they trained, who were able to take down their best fighter and one of their secret weapons, they wouldn't count on us working together to do this.

The training made sure of that.

"Hell yeah!" Drew said, her face no longer scrunched up. "If it's us, we've got this."

Yeah, we did have this. Thinking it through logically always brought me to the same conclusion - we had an advantage over the Academy. After being able to fend off their first attack in such a dominating manner, we now had the advantage. They had lost their intel and we still had the element of surprise. Whatever we did first would be a success, it's what comes after that would decide the rest of the battle. We were only two people and they had an army specially trained for fighting. It wouldn't be easy. Either one of us could die at any time because of a minor slip up. They could predict what we were planning, however unlikely it was, because sometimes these things happen.

However, I did know one thing. We were going to try everything. We weren't going to give up and we would never stop fighting no matter how much we wanted to or how much we lost. We would complete this mission no matter what and not let anyone get in our way. We would take down the Academy, and stop them committing all the heinous acts that they continually perpetrate. We would either stop the Academy or die trying. Either way, we wouldn't let any of them escape without being punished, and for that, we needed people who would carry on our task even if we died. People who held the same belief about the Academy as us. People who would fight for our cause until the end, or, in other words, new recruits which was going to be very hard.,

But, well, you know how the saying goes, "Out of the frying pan and into the fire."

CHAPTER 7

My lungs burned as I sprinted through the hallway. There were too many to fight alone. On top of all that, Ana was chasing me too. I had lost my headset earlier so there was no one I could speak with, which was even more nerve-wracking. I had been relying on that to aid my hasty egress. Not having it anymore was a massive handicap and I knew it. The hallway I was running through felt endless. I wasn't sure how much longer I could keep running at this pace. The pain in my lungs increased as I pushed as hard as I could. Ending it here would result in everyone I cared about becoming vulnerable again and I needed to avoid that at all costs. The twists and turns in this place made it hard to keep track of where I was going but I persevered, adamant about getting out. Although I had memorised the parts of the Academy that I had been in, the fact that I was going in and out of uncharted territory made accomplishing my goal that much harder. If I wasn't as good as I was at mapping an area while going through it, I would've either got lost or been caught a long time ago.

It was surprising to see how many rooms there were that I hadn't seen before today that were so important to this place. The upgraded training room that looked brand new and unused and the massive halls that put the small one's downstairs to shame. It looked like they were going for an upgrade, and for that, they would need more girls. They would need to take more people. More people that they would then mess up physically and mentally with all their malicious tactics used to break people in.

Getting out was my top priority but it wouldn't hurt to check some of these rooms and memorise where they were for any future plans regarding this place. However, first and foremost, I needed to get out safely, which was turning into a much bigger hassle than I had previously thought it would be. I should've had a back-up plan. Not having one could result in my downfall right here and now.

Finally seeing the end of the hallway, I pushed that bit more, exiting the facility, and appearing out into the open. The cold air hit me as I slowed my pace just a little bit to be quieter. I also needed to catch my breath so that I wasn't making too much noise. You never knew who was going to be listening. As it was dark, I had many options of where to hide, but considering how close they were behind me, I needed to get into the shadows as quickly as possible.

Finally settling on my decision to go into the tree line, I blended into the shadows, vanishing out of immediate sight. Around me were a lot of trees but a path lay in the middle, separating them from each other. The only man-made thing apart from that was an abandoned building that I could see in the distance. It was quite far away but if I could get to it, I could hide well enough to make them continue looking for me elsewhere.

I was getting away, but slowly, as they were combing the forest meticulously, which slowed them down considerably. Unfortunately for me, one of them had gone ahead of the others and was nearly on me. As I had caught my breath, I knew that I would be able to outrun her but, I wanted them to slow down even more and the best way to get them to do that was to show them how dangerous I actually was.

Hiding behind a tree, I waited for the girl to pass by. I had slowed my breathing down completely and made sure to plot a path with no leaves. Within a few seconds she had passed right by the tree I was behind, obviously not paying much attention to her surroundings. Ignoring the threat that I posed would be their downfall. As she flew past, I stuck my arm out, hitting her right in the throat. Her legs came flying out in front of her and she flopped to the floor. As she started trying to catch her breath, I quickly bent down to her level and sliced her throat open to stop her calling out for help. For them to be afraid of me I needed to do more.

I started wildly stabbing her at random not paying attention to where the knife was going. It didn't take more than a few seconds for her to stop moving but I continued for a few seconds more to make it look as gruesome as possible, before wiping my knife in the leaves and carrying on ahead. I left her body in plain sight for everyone to see, grimacing at the actions I had to take to get what I wanted.

The dilapidated building was upon me before I knew it. Cautiously entering, I did a quick check of the house to make sure that no one was in here and that I knew the layout as best I could.

Outside, I heard the moment that the girls found the body of their fallen friend. None of them seemed to have the stomach to go on, which benefitted me greatly.

All I had to worry about now was the biggest threat of them all. Ana Rodriguez.

She had mentioned once before how she was one of the people who helped start this Academy. One of the trainees to be precise. So, her skills would be a lot higher than all of those Academy girls put together. Having that much time to refine your craft and perfect it allowed for much greater control and precision.

I hadn't heard her with the other girls and I had stayed by the broken window the whole time, so she must be somewhere else entirely.

Just as that thought crossed my mind, my head, which was out the window, suddenly had cold hard metal pressed against it.

"Don't move," Ana said, coolly, "Or I will shoot."

I didn't feel any fear, but I froze anyway. I listened to her advice, but I couldn't stop thinking about all the things that had brought me to this day.

"It's sad," She was saying, a sigh in her voice. "You had so much potential."

I stayed silent, not wanting to provoke her at all.

"Well," She said, suddenly cold again. "I would apologise, but I am not sorry at all."

A gun shot rang out, signalling the end the journey.

Part Two

CHAPTER 8

12 Days Earlier

Drew and I had been tracking down some people we wanted to add to our team. As we were only two, there was only so much we could do - only so many jobs that we could divide between ourselves. Having someone who was on a computer looking at schematics or the cameras and trying to help from that angle would only leave one person on the ground, and that person could easily be overwhelmed by the sheer numbers the Academy had on their side.

We were looking into a group that wasn't well known, even in the underworld, but by going on some chat rooms on the deep web we had been able to deduce that they had done a lot of jobs that others had claimed credit for. Since they didn't want to be known they had let others claim them freely. As some of the best in the business, they wouldn't just help us because we asked, especially since this was much bigger than anything they had ever done before. We would have to have some sort of payment or offer we could give them.

Luckily for us, we had something that they would want: Information. One of them had a sister who had been taken by the Academy recently so she would be able to get her sister out safely if we acted quickly. Since we knew where the Academy was, we could give that information and our help in exchange for them helping us. It was a solid basis to start from. Since they were unlikely to believe us or even take us mildly seriously, we decided to interrupt them in the middle of a job.

We found their getaway car and got into it as it was probably easiest to talk to them after they had made their escape. Of course, without them knowing.

"Come on!" One of them said. "Do it quicker!"

They seemed to be rushing a little bit.

It wasn't long before the one inside flew out the back door and over to their car. All three jumped in sped and away, leaving the people that were chasing them behind.

"What did you do Vanessa?!" The guy, Adam, asked the girl who had been in the building.

"Leave her alone!" The other girl, Lucy, said. "It was different from how we thought it was going to be."

"Yeah Adam," Vanessa said in a bored tone. "Now get off my case."

These were the three that comprised the group.

Adam, the computer specialist that didn't fit the stereotype at all. Short dark brown hair that brought his features out perfectly. His clothes, very casual, composed of just jeans and a plain T-Shirt. His face was very expressive and he seemed very loud.

Vanessa was their close combat specialist. The one who was usually on the field alone, seemed very calm and hard to get to elicit any emotion. Her long flowing, glossy black hair framed her sharp features and cold glare that she wore constantly. Her outfit was made up of black on black. From her long-sleeved top to her running shoes - all of it was black. She even had on a black mask that she had just taken off as she entered the car.

Last, but not least, was the one whose sibling had been taken. Lucy. She was their designated sharpshooter, a sniper if you will. One of the best in the business from her track record. Light brown hair surrounded her soft, kind features, bringing out her bright blue eyes. She was wearing a skin-tight leather suit but had a wool bodywarmer over it. She had been stationed outside the car but hadn't noticed as we sneaked inside it. Her concerned look proved that our research into their personalities had been successful. She, like the rest of the group, was one of the founders. They had another member but that was her sister, who, as we knew, was taken.

Our research into them had paid off because the character descriptions we had come up with were looking very accurate. As we listened to their conversation that confirmed our thoughts, the only thing left to do was to make them notice us.

"Hey," I said coolly.

"Ahhh!" Lucy screamed as she jumped and turned around.

The others turned around too but more casually.

"What the fuck?!" Adam half-shouted. "Who the hell are you guys?!"

"We're here to help," I said, trying to add a calming tone to my voice.

"Why are you in our car?" Vanessa said deadpan, glaring at Lucy. "In fact, how did you get in here. I thought Lucy was watching over the car."

"Eh? Don't look at me!" Lucy said, turning away from us. "It isn't my fault that I'm not good in the field."

"How many times do I have to tell you," Vanessa said, sighing. "You can't only be good at one thing."

"Uh, guys?" Adam said, looking incredulously at the girls. "You can fight later, but why are we just ignoring the fact that we have two people chilling in our car?"

"Oh," Lucy said, looking embarrassed. "Right."

"So, what the hell are you guys doing in here," Vanessa said. She had already pulled out her weapon before but was now pointing it at us. "Or do we have to take you out."

I'd like to see you try, I thought.

"As I said, we're here to help." Drew and I put our hands up, which visibly put them at ease.

"Help with what?" Lucy questioned. Looking very interested.

"With your sister." I said, answering her question.

"My sister?" Lucy questioned. "What about her."

"We can help you get her back."

"Wait, really?" Her tone changed from suspicion to excitement instantly.

Wow, this girl trusted others way too fast, but I guess that was good for us now, wasn't it?

"Yes," I said, continuing on. "Although we will need your help with something in exchange. You understand, right?"

"You can really help get my sister back?" Lucy questioned, hopefully.

"Oh please," Vanessa said, rolling her eyes. "They can't help for shit."

"Yeah," Adam said putting his focus back on driving. "Let's just kick them out and get on with it."

"Wait!" Lucy said, turning to her friends. "What if they actually know where she is?"

"We do know where your sister is," I said. "Where Isabella is."

Mentioning her name would help a lot as Lucy had Adam do a lot of work to wipe her existence from all systems, probably done to protect her. They had done a really good job. Not even me or Drew could find anything about her online. Knowing her name meant that we knew about her, and the only way in which we could possibly know that was by having met her in real life.

Lucy looked at me wide-eyed, and even Vanessa and Adam looked surprised. I guess it was the right choice to mention Isabella's name then!

Mentioning Isabella's name had convinced Lucy enough. Although the others didn't trust us much, they still trusted Lucy's judgment on this decision. When we mentioned what we needed their help for they were more than happy to help out. Their morals probably wouldn't let them turn it down. We hadn't told them that Isabella was inside the Academy. We were going to do that after we had confirmed that they knew of our skills.

They had planned a mission, one of the hardest that they could come up with, and we would have to complete it. This mission was a lot easier than all of the ones I had done so far, but I wasn't going to tell them that. It comprised of breaking into a facility and stealing some information. They didn't provide any more information other than where the place was and what we were trying to steal. Luckily, we were very well versed in the art of finding out information that wasn't publicly available.

"Okay, we've got everything ready," Adam said. "It's go time."

Vanessa rolled her eyes at his words but sent us off.

Lucy looked anxious. She didn't know how well trained we were so that would be a welcome surprise.

"Well," I said, pausing. "We'll be back soon."

We quickly exited the place they had us hiding out in and went quietly towards the place we were supposed to break into. It was a small building width-wise, but it was tall. It didn't take us much time to break in through one of the windows. Climbing up this high was second nature. No one was around so we didn't have to worry about people seeing us. Only cameras and sensors. We had already mapped out where all the cameras were and because this wasn't a newer building, luckily, the only way to set a sensor off was by either going in line of sight of one of the cameras (we were avoiding this already) or opening doors without first swiping the key card.

I had recreated the key card and it worked perfectly, as I knew it would.

While I kept watch, Drew easily found and downloaded the files.

We slipped out into the night, leaving no trace that we were ever there.

As we arrived back, Lucy, Vanessa, and Adam looked at us surprised.

"You're back already?" Vanessa asked, sounding confused.

"It wasn't hard," Drew said, indicating the USB with the information we had gone in to get.

"So, what are the files that we brought back going to be used for?" I asked.

We knew what was on the USB - schematics for a building - but we didn't know why or what the building was and what it had to do with us.

"Well, you see..." Adam trailed off.

"It's for the equipment that we thought you guys would need." Vanessa carried on. "But, after seeing how efficient you are, I guess if anyone needs it, it is us!"

I was quite surprised that they had thought that far ahead. Because of how goofily they acted, I kind of just forgot that they were one of the best at what they did. Planning ahead was always a necessity. Even if it didn't turn out how it was supposed to, it was still better to have a plan that failed than not have one at all as it would make it harder in every way.

Lucy still looked shocked that we had done it so quickly. She was definitely the least experienced out of everyone on this team because she didn't have as many high-pressure situations to deal with, unlike the other two.

Breaking and entering into a place and stealing something would give most, especially when starting out, a massive rush of adrenaline. After a while it calms down, but that's only when one is comfortable with the situation, and that takes different amounts of time, depending on the person.

Hacking and monitoring the situation would put anyone under a lot of stress straight away. You would have to be precise with your hacking but also extremely fast because of the stressful conditions. Monitoring the situation would require a good grasp on all areas so that quick and precise instructions on how to move around in the most efficient manner could be given.

Meanwhile, Lucy had been sitting back waiting for opportunities to pick people off. This was all done from relative safety as she usually stayed quite far away, only moving close when they had to leave by car. This didn't allow her to get proper experience working in the field or in high-intensity situations, because, although snipers would usually be put under this kind of stress when going to take the shot, she had never been in an actual situation where she had to take a shot. She was trained, became highly skilled using a sniper, and was always there just in case, but she had never actually taken the shot and killed someone. That could prove to be a problem in the future but there wasn't really much we could do about that. It was situation-based, and all circumstances change, which meant that she didn't have the luxury of having much prior experience. It would've been nice if we could've had an experienced sniper backing us up but we had to make do with what we had, and the others, while not on mine and Drew's level, were very competent and handy to have in our team.

Now that we had completed the mission and they had seen how skilled we were, I knew it was now time for us to tell them about where Lucy's sister, Isabella, was being kept and what we wanted them to help us with. But that could wait for tomorrow. Right now, all I wanted to do was sleep. It felt like I hadn't in a long time.

Waking up fully rested, I was ready to tell them all about the Academy. Gathering everyone in one room, I started, Drew by my side.

"The Academy is a place where Drew and I had been held for months," I said, their faces already showing surprise. "That is where we learned all we know. All of our skills in different mediums that are used to break in and enter places."

"The Academy is where Isabella is being held," Drew added.

"How do you know she is there?" Lucy asked. "Did you see her?"

"Yes, we did see her," I answered. "She was always by herself and not surrounded by anyone else, which, in there, is very unusual. In there, you'd be better off surrounding yourself with as many people as possible to avoid getting attacked and being outnumbered, or, to avoid special 'training sessions' that were basically just torture sessions to get the girls huddled up together so that picking a partner that they worked well with was easy."

Lucy looked stricken and I could understand why. The Academy was hell, and her sister was going through it all and there was nothing she could do to stop it.

"So how are we going to get into the Academy?" Adam asked.

"We've already made a plan," I said. "Which is why we need you guys for it. The more numbers, the higher the chance of success."

Quickly going over the plan that we had made, we got them to agree to it. They seemed very happy with the plan and confident that it would work.

"So, this place is just filled with girls?" Vanessa asked, afterwards. "If so, that is kind of weird."

I never knew the reason for this and so I looked up at Drew, wondering if she had the answer.

"The reason that it is all girls is pretty simple. They can be used in more situations. From the normal assassination, to infiltration by becoming close to either people that know the target or the target themselves. They can also use their bodies more effectively compared to males." Drew answered. "Men taken and trained would have less of a chance at a few of those things, although they would still definitely excel at the normal, assassination, killing or execution."

That did make sense. More variety meant fewer requirements for more people and being able to save not only space but also the money spent by just getting girls was a smart and well thought out decision.

"Makes sense," Vanessa said, leaning back in her chair.

Now, we needed to move onto the next part - getting the equipment we needed.

Firstly, we needed some clothes that blended in with the surroundings. Once we were inside, they would be useless, but outside, they would help a lot. It was crucial to get them before the mission.

We all already had our weapons or things that we used for the mission. I had my daggers and Drew had her sword. Vanessa had her knife, which she was always playing with,

Adam had his computer rig set up to be fully transportable and Lucy had her sniper. She told me she had been using it since they first set up. Getting black clothes was our next priority and so Drew and I quickly went out and got some. The material was stretchy so it allowed for freedom for us to choose the correct sizes.

Next, we needed a map of the building. Drew and I could picture its layout in our heads but Vanessa, Lucy, and Adam had no idea what it looked like so our plan wouldn't make any sense to them. Drawing some of the floors and the main living areas with Drew was easy. We couldn't draw the whole building as we never had full access it when we were there, but it was enough to be able to make a plan reliably without the chance of much going wrong. Things never went exactly to plan so I would've liked to have had more information but, we had to work with what we had.

Now being able to see our plan designed on paper allowed the group to better understand and become more comfortable with it. Our plan relied a lot on me so I was going to have to train a lot in the coming days to be ready for this.

We had decided to infiltrate the facility in exactly eight days. So, we didn't have much time to plan, but time was key in this situation as Lucy was worried about what they were going to try to do to Isabella. We also had our own motives for going in this early. It would give Ana less time to plan and get everything ready. When we were there, we had been told about emergency situations and what to do when called upon. It took two weeks for them to set everything up. Specifically, fourteen days from when they (the enemy) attacked us and we killed them.

Not being able to get in contact with two of their best would put them in a high alert situation and make them prepare for the setup. We had taken a day to track down and find this group, which meant that we now had thirteen days until they went into the special lockdown/high alert mode. So, we had twelve days to infiltrate this place. If we didn't do it before then we weren't going to be able to do it any other time. But right now, what I needed to focus on was training. I wouldn't allow myself to be the reason we failed the mission. Of course, I didn't want anybody else to, but I would be most disappointed if it was my error that caused it. So, my full focus up until the mission day would be just training. I wouldn't allow any other variable.

Day four, like all the other days, consisted mainly of training. I was focusing on training with Drew right now as she had the most experience, especially against me, but I also wanted to try training against Vanessa too. She wasn't really as good as me but it would not only boost her abilities but also allow me to make sure I had it down fully as I'd be teaching someone else. It would reinforce my knowledge and technique. Fighting with Drew now was so much easier than before. I could actually put up a really good fight when she was trying her hardest, which was a stark change from what it used to be.

"You've improved so much." Drew said, breathlessly.

"It's all down to your training." I said, trying to catch my breath while not letting down my guard.

"You're the one who was always focused and willing to learn new things," Drew said, starting to come towards me again. "You deserve most of the credit."

She lunged at me, trying to catch me off guard with her speed, but I didn't allow that to phase me. Going on the counter, I darted inside her guard as she had overextended, and tried to land a body shot but, as she was Drew, she was able to twist her body in such a way that it allowed her to dodge my punch. Only Drew would be capable of doing something like that while being that much off balance.

We continued trading blows, trying to actually land a meaningful shot on each other but no matter what both of us tried, we seemed to be at a stalemate.

Drew and I dropped to the ground at the same time. No one had been able to win the fight and since we had been going at it for nearly an hour without any breaks, we were struggling to stand upright. Not even superhuman people like Drew would be able to withstand such training without becoming thoroughly tired.

"We really are evenly matched now, aren't we?" Drew said, after we had caught out breath.

"You're still a bit ahead of me." I answered back.

She had landed more hits on me and if the fight had carried on without either of us losing stamina it would've been Drew's win.

"Maybe," Drew said, unconvinced. "That's enough for today, we can carry on tomorrow."

"Okay." I answered. I wanted to carry on more but I knew that Drew would only say that because she had something important to do and so I left it.

Thinking about what to do led me to realise that now I didn't just have Drew to train with. Vanessa was another fighter in here and it would give me a very good chance to see her skills first hand. She was described as a good fighter but lacked a lot. So, if I could also help her here it would be a massive boost to our team as a whole.

"Vanessa!" I called out, walking up to her.

"What do you want." The distrust was still clear on her face.

It was understandable that she still didn't trust us. We had only known each other for a few days now. In fact, it was weirder that Adam and Lucy, especially, were able to trust us in such a short amount of time. In the end, it did help us a lot as Lucy and Adam were on board with our plan straight away.

While not trusting us was the right response, we needed that trust for her to fully commit to the mission.

"Want to train?" I asked her.

She raised her eyebrow, looking sceptically at me.

"Drew is doing something else and I can't spar with either Lucy or Adam." I carried on.

"Okay, I'll spar with you." Still staring at me like I was a weirdo, she had answered.

"So, we'll spar with no weapons then. Only fists." I said, getting warmed up.

"Mhm." Vanessa said, doing the same opposite me.

A few minutes later we were both warmed up and had started to fight.

The first thing I noticed was that she was very slow. She seemed to struggle to make decisions on what to do when fighting. She must've not had many people to practise with because that was something that was developed from fighting opponents with different styles and different movements. You could study it as much as you wanted, but once you actually got into a fight it was much harder to implement the decisions, especially in such a tight time constraint.

Because of that hesitation in her decision making, although she used her whole body well when striking, she lacked the full power that confidence brought.

All of this resulted in me easily being able to subdue her and win the fight.

"When did you start fighting and how did you learn?" I asked her. I didn't want to tell her the flaws in her form and fighting straight away. I wanted her to trust me first.

"Probably way after you." She said, reluctantly. Hesitating again, she finally answered properly. "It's been just under a year and I learn on my own."

That explained it. She didn't have the luxury of having someone else of equal or above skill level. This resulted in her not having anyone to tell her when and how she was going wrong or have the experience of growing at the same rate with another person.

"I started just under a year too."

"Seriously?" She said, sounding shocked. "And you're this good?"

"I mean, when all you're forced to do is take beatings and fight every day you don't really have any choice." I said, smiling sadly.

She looked at me as if she was seeing me for the first time. A renewed look of respect was plastered on her face. When we continued our sparring it looked like some of the hesitancy had been flushed out her system. She could be a really good fighter one day. Before we knew it, we had finished up and Vanessa had left. I was just leaving when I saw Lucy sitting with her arms around her legs, knees drawn to her chest.

"Lucy?" I said, shocked by her sudden appearance.

By the look on her face she was out of it. Thinking about all the things that could cause this and why she would come to the training room, the only thing that came to mind was she was really worried about her sister, and considering I knew how it was in there, it didn't surprise me at all that she had come to me - once I had thought about it.

"I wanted to talk to you more about my sister." She said, looking really hopefully at me.

I had been correct.

"Sure, let's go back to my room."

What I was calling my room was more of a small box shaped closet that didn't have anything in it but an old mattress with no sheet or duvet and some drawers.

Putting my clothes into the little chest of drawers that I had, I sat down, inviting Lucy to do the same.

"So, what did you want to know about her?" I asked once she had sat down.

"It's not really just about my sister..." She said frantically, playing with her fingers. "It's more about how she will be treated there."

"She won't be treated well at all." I said bluntly, and saw her face fall. "I'm not going to sugar coat the situation that she will be in because it is a very dangerous one. It all really depends on how she acts; whether she obeys or if she doesn't."

"She isn't the kind that likes to disobey the people who have an advantage over she. She is more of a follower." Lucy said. "Does that mean that she will be fine?"

"You can never be fine in a place like that." A look of despair overcame her face but I carried on. "But if she doesn't go against what they're saying and follows their orders, she will still be alive and not too worse for wear."

That final part seemed to calm her mind somewhat and stop her going over most of the bad things she thought were going to happen. No one could guarantee her safety, but if all that Lucy was telling me was true, then she wouldn't have any problems physically surviving.

"What about her physical condition?" I asked, but seeing her confused face, I clarified. "Does she have a lot of stamina and does she have any experience with fighting?"

"She loved running so I'd say she has pretty decent stamina, but she hasn't taken any classes or had any first-hand experience with fighting." Lucy said. "Is that a bad thing?"

"Not being able to fight is pretty bad but it will only leave a few more bruises on her compared to normal." I answered. "But compared to lacking stamina it isn't noteworthy at all. That stamina will help your sister so much."

"Thanks for answering my questions." Lucy said, getting up.

The look on her face was one of determination and slight relief. Compared to how she looked when she first came into my room, it was a stark difference. It seemed that now she was fully really to do anything for her sister and confident that she was still alive and kicking. This resolve would only help her when it came down to the final part of our plan.

Lucy left the room and I lay down, exhausted. I had done a lot of training today and needed to sleep, if only for a bit. Closing my eyes, I felt the tension ebb, reducing itself to nothingness.

Waking up, I felt completely refreshed. No longer did I feel the fatigue from earlier wracking my body. Checking the time, I realised why. While I had only wanted to take a quick nap, I had ended up sleeping for a whole day. Well, nothing I could do about it now. Anyway, today was the day that I wanted to leave for the Academy. We wouldn't be able to get close as they had a lot of guards outside, but if we played our cards right, we might find something that wasn't on the map or something we hadn't seen before.

Getting up, I went into the main room and luckily everyone was already there. As I entered all of them looked towards me.

"We're leaving today." I said.

"For the Academy?" Adam asked.

"Yes."

Apart from Drew, they all looked a bit shocked.

"Why so early?" Vanessa asked.

"Because it's better to get used to the factors that we can't control in our current situation," Drew answered, stepping in for me. "Like the weather. It's a lot harder to run further in the rain and cold or the heat, compared to if the weather is just normal and stable."

They all nodded, seeming to get the reason and not having any objections to it.

"So, should we get all the things ready?" Lucy asked, standing up and getting ready to leave the room."

"Yes," I said. "Forgetting anything will be detrimental to us."

As Lucy left the room, Vanessa got up too. Sarcastically saluting at me before following.

Adam got back to his work as he was trying to find a way for us to get there.

"No need to do that." I said, "Drew and I have thought of a way we can do that already."

"How?" Adam asked. Curiosity filling his face.

"We will impersonate a private jet owner and steal it so that we can get there quickly." I said. "Since it is only a short trip, we should be off and disappeared before anyone has the chance to discover that we aren't who we say we are."

"So, all I need to do is make fake passports for a few rich people that have their jet at the nearest airport to us?" Adam asked, his face filling with excitement. "I've always wanted to do something like this. It'll be a piece of cake."

Just before his fingers touched the keyboard, he froze, turning towards us.

"Who is going to fly the plane?" He asked hesitantly.

"I am." Drew replied confidently.

"This is so nerve wracking." Lucy said after we had gone past airport security.

With no surprise to anyone, the fake credentials that Adam had come up with worked like a charm, getting us through with no problems.

"Were you doubting me?" Adam said mockingly.

"No!" Lucy hissed. "That's not what I meant."

"Guys, fight on the plane but not now. We aren't properly through yet." Vanessa said, an exasperated look on her face.

Although a fuss hadn't started with anyone else, the animated conversation had still got quite a lot of people to look over to us, curious as to what was going on.

Drew and I were in front walking confidently. Since we were the most level-headed and both had a way with our words, everyone volunteered us to be the ones handling all conversations to get us past the security. Finally getting past all checkpoints, we entered the jet. While the rest of the group explored the plane, I kept Drew company while she got things ready. She looked in her element. Even when talking to the air traffic controllers there was no difficulty. She was able to use all the terminology that I had no clue would be useful or needed. It was really lucky that we had someone as talented as this on our side.

"You're really good at this." I mentioned to her once we had taken off.

"Well, the experiences that I've had flying planes didn't allow any room for error." She said. "We went straight to flying actual planes, no simulation."

She had briefly mentioned how she had got to the point of being able to fly planes and I had thought that she had had some training in the simulators they use for teaching, but I guess Drew was even more impressive than I thought.

"Are you sure everyone is going to be ready for this mission?" Drew asked a few minutes later.

I thought about it for a bit. Would they actually be ready? Probably not.

All we could do was get them as close to ready as possible and hope that they could step up in the end. There wasn't anything else for us to do apart from that, unfortunately.

Vanessa, the one who had the most experience infiltrating buildings, was nowhere near as good as either me or Drew. She lacked experience in her fighting and from what I had seen of her, the thing she lacked most was the ability to think on the fly. It may not seem that important but being able to do that gave a massive advantage as you were able to adapt and overcome bad circumstances very quickly and efficiently.

With Adam, he was a lot better with computers compared to me but when compared to Drew he was only a little better, making his position kind of obsolete. The main advantage of bringing him with us was to allow Drew to be with me as we worked best together. So, he was useful, but not as much as the last member of the team.

Lucy was our most important member, but also, unfortunately, the least experienced of the three. Her presence as a sniper was crucial to our plan but both Drew and I were going to have to spend the most time helping her.

"I'm not sure." I said, sighing. "But we have to get them as close as possible."

Drew nodded back, seeming to share the same train of thought as me.

The rest of the plane ride went by quickly. Drew and I shared mostly idle chatter as it wasn't going to be long until we landed again. We also decided that as soon as we found somewhere to stay, we were going to start training them all to get better at using their weapons (expect Adam, as we didn't know anything from his field that he didn't know already, although we were going to train him in a bit of self-defence).

Drew, again, perfectly communicated with the ground crew so that we could land safely.

As we landed, I went into the area that the rest of the group were to tell them what we had both decided.

On entering, they all looked up at me, seeming to sense that I was about to say something.

"Listen up." I said, making sure that they knew this was important. "We're going to train you guys harder than you've ever been trained before as soon as we find somewhere to stay."

When I had finished, they had three different expressions on their faces. Vanessa looked determined. I liked the look of hunger to improve on her face. It would make that process much quicker. Adam looked annoyed, but as soon as I looked towards him that expression dropped off his face, leaving him looking sheepish. Meanwhile, Lucy looked defeated. Like she had no belief in herself to improve in such a short space of time.

By the end of the first day I was going to try and get them all ready for the training. Being mentally prepared was as important as getting physically prepared in situations with as much pressure as this one.

"You understand?" I said, making sure that the weight of my words reached them.

"We're ready." They said together, their different tones being easy identifiable.

The next few days were going to be hard for them but what good thing wasn't at least a bit hard?

It had been a few days since our training had started but the difference in them was already outstanding.

Vanessa was a lot better with hand to hand combat. Simulating situations where she needed to think on her feet got her more experienced and had allowed more confidence to be instilled in her. Adam could now sufficiently defend himself easily against a casual person, although he would never be a match for any of the girls in the Academy. Lucy, unfortunately, was still struggling. Her confidence had only risen a little bit since we first started training. It was like she had reverted to the person I saw when we first met them. I could only think of a few things to help her and one of them was fighting. I wasn't sure if it would help but blowing off steam this way and reassuring myself that I was capable of protecting not only me but others had always helped out. I only hoped that it was a help to reassure her that her sister was going to be fine.

CHAPTER 9

Isabella

"Move faster!" I heard one of the instructors say from behind me before a girl cried out.

My heart leapt hearing this, spurring me on and forcing me to not look behind. I was scared. So, so scared. I was so extremely petrified that all I could do was follow orders and hoped others would do the same, but some were insane and disobeyed the people in charge. Those people were either getting 'treatment' with the doctor or their bodies had already been disposed of.

They always made us watch their executions or beatings and I would never be able to get used to that kind of violence.

If only I hadn't gone out on my own that late at night and had listened to my sister. Then I wouldn't be in this situation. I wouldn't be missing her as much as I did. I would probably never be able to get out of here. I had already resigned myself to staying here, unable to do anything to get out. After seeing all I'd seen, anyone would think the same thing.

"And time!" The instructor said, signalling for us to stop running.

We all quickly lined up, as routine, and stayed deathly quiet.

"We need better," The instructor said, raking over us with her ferocious gaze. "If I call out your name, come and see me."

As soon as she started calling out names, I stopped listening. Since I had done very well this session, I knew that I wasn't going to be called out anytime soon.

I didn't have any friends here so listening for the names called was pointless. It was nothing more than a waste of time.

What I actually needed to focus on was my fighting. While I was always doing well in the fitness part of this torture, I needed to learn how to fight properly and take their lessons on board, otherwise I was going to be left behind and forgotten. While I didn't think I was ever going to get out I did know someone who wouldn't ever give up on me.

My sister, Lucy. She had always been there for me, helping me, looking out for me, never letting me down and she always would. If she wasn't my sister, I think I would've given up all hope and let myself die already, but, because I knew her, I had the smallest slither of hope.

That small slither was extended when two well-known people suddenly escaped. Their names were Drew and Katie. They had disappeared, and at first, I thought that they had been killed off but after a while, I overheard one of the people in charge talking about their escape and how they needed to recapture them before they made any move against the Academy. No one else knew about this and I'd never tell anyone I knew; the risk wasn't worth it.

"Go back to your rooms," the pedagogue said. "It's the end of the day."

We all moved quickly after hearing this, not wanting to stick around any longer than necessary. Weaving through the throng of people I made it back to my room in no time and sat down on the bed. Although this was the best part of the day - no training, no pain, and a smaller amount of fear - I still didn't enjoy it at all.

The hours of silence with nobody to talk to. I had tried to make friends with one of the girls here, but she ended up getting beaten and distanced herself from everyone afterwards. The girl I knew before no longer remained and I didn't recognise who she had become at all. This experience tore me apart and had stopped me from making any other friends while stuck in here. Since then, I had been on my own, trying to survive with no one's help. I had wanted to try and make friends but every time I even got close to someone else, I felt the panic start to set in and ended up not doing anything. I was not sure if I would ever be able to make friends again.

I was constantly bored and had to remain thinking about things, otherwise I was not sure how I would cope, from the small, cold concrete rooms, to the thick metal doors, and even to the little, tiny bed pushed into the corner of the room. This was not a place made for any sort of comfort. It felt like it was meant to be as uncomfortable as possible while not being unbearable. It was close to making me lose my mind.

Lucy, being the only thing that was keeping me moving, was on my mind constantly. I always thought about her to calm myself down, keep myself busy. Drowning my worries with thoughts of her always managed to calm me down enough.

All I wanted was to see her again. To apologise for not listening to her. For going out at that time. All of it. All of it was, and will always be, my biggest regret. But, as I'd been hearing new things, I'd realised one thing. The Academy didn't let just anyone in. They were known for how thoroughly they scouted all the people here before kidnapping them and making them into assassins. If I hadn't gone out that night, they would have still got me, except since my sister would have been there, and would have defended me, I knew that she would have been hurt or even killed, getting in their way. Since Vanessa was the only competent fighter and she wasn't there, we wouldn't have stood a chance.

All I could do was my best every day, hoping that maybe, just maybe, one day, I would be able to get out of this place. If that day ever came, I would actually appreciate life more than I did before. Freedom was something that Lucy ensured and something that I took for granted. I would never make that mistake again if I ever got the chance to have a life again. As I drifted off into the depths of sleep, the only thing on my mind was Lucy.

"Please Lucy...please help..." Before my consciousness drifted off into the unknown.

CHAPTER 10

Katie

It was finally the day. Now or never. We wouldn't get another chance at this, so we had to make sure that everything was perfect. If something went horribly wrong, we would all be dead before we even realised it. We had travelled to the base and were now waiting a few miles away as we didn't want to risk being spotted at all. That would be the most anticlimactic ending to our journey.

"Lucy, Adam," I said with a pause. "We'll be going now."

"See ya!" Adam said with a lazy wave, fully focused on his laptop.

"Be careful." Lucy said, still seeming to be as worried as she was before we got here.

Giving Drew a look to let her know what I was going to do, I went over to Lucy and took her from the group so that we could speak.

"What is it that has been bothering you since we landed in this place?" I asked in a gentle voice.

"It's just..." She trailed off before continuing. "It's just that we're so close now. What if we fail?"

Her concern was normal. In fact, the lack of nerves surrounding the majority of us was the unusual part in all of this.

"Do you trust me?" I asked Lucy, looking into her eyes.

"I do." She said quietly, looking down.

"Then trust in this," I put my hands on her shoulders, startling her and making her look up. "I am going to do everything possible to get your sister back. Nothing is going to be able to stop me. Everyone is going to be safe, and after today, you won't have to worry about the Academy taking your sister or doing anything to her ever again, you understand?"

I had this confidence in myself that hadn't gone away since I had left here. Quite the opposite had occurred actually. The unyielding confidence that I did have was as a result of the affirmation of my strength compared to another who had more training and experience in the same place. That person being Matilda, Blake's sister, who had tried to kill me.

Lucy kept glancing around my face after I had finished my statement, like she was looking for something. A few moments later she found it and a resolute look appeared in her eyes.

"We are going to get Isabella back." She said, strongly and clearly.

Compared to the tone that she had portrayed more often in the past, she finally sounded like she believed that we were going to succeed, rather than just going along with what we said, like a kid to a parent.

I stood up in front of everyone getting ready to speak before the mission after realising that they could be feeling somewhat similar to Lucy, expect for different reasons, to give them more confidence and make them feel more at ease. Although I had expected Drew to become the leader of the team as she had been my mentor and knew more than me about most things to do with the Academy and things related to that, to my surprise, I had become the leader of this de facto, leader of this mismatching, ragtag group of hard working, inexperienced recruits. I had slipped right into this role, not even asking Drew if she had wanted to be the one to lead, but she never mentioned anything about that situation. In fact, knowing her personality, she would be delighted to not have to lead a group of people as that required a lot of talking and Drew was like the animal that disliked humans the most, being, well, humans themselves.

"You all know the plan; everything has been spoken about hundreds of times already, so you don't need me to speak about that." I said, pausing, before carrying on. "But what I will say is that all of you have a lot more ability than you believe, and I've trained you, and seen you in action so I would know. This mission won't be easy but if you follow the plan and have trust in yourselves and each other, it will be a breeze."

After I had finished speaking, I looked around to make sure that everyone had heard my words, but what I saw when I looked shocked me. Instead of looking like they were bored like I had thought, both Vanessa and Adam, the ones who I thought were going to be dismissive of my speech, looked on; entranced. Their usual sarcastic and distracted looks were no longer there. Instead they looked serious. Their eyes shone, belief clear beneath the surface.

"Now it's actually time to go." I said, splitting everyone into teams.

Firstly, was me, Drew, and Vanessa. The three of us were going to infiltrate the base together. Next was Adam, who was going to stay nearby to the place we had waited all this time and finally Lucy, who was going to stay with Adam as they both played a very, very important roles in our mission.

Leaving those two behind, Drew, Vanessa and I left to go towards the entrance of the Academy. Once we got close enough, I was able to see the building that had haunted so many of my nightmares. This was the building that started everything. The one we were now going to take down.

Two guards stood outside the door. They were actual armed guards so we wouldn't be able to just run up to them and take them down that way. We had to sneak up behind them to make sure that this part went without a hitch. Indicating to Vanessa, who was in between me and Drew, to make a noise so both of us on either side of her could creep in the opposite direction, flanking the guards. Once they had heard the noise they listened for a bit before shouting out, telling whoever was there to come out. Of course, Vanessa didn't listen to their "requests" and stayed hidden in the tree line. Finally, sensing that they weren't going to get anywhere with just talking, one of the guards slowly walked towards where Vanessa was hiding. Once that guard had got a good distance away from the other, I signalled to Drew to take him down. Meanwhile, I would deal with the other one.

Drew took down her target and I blended into the shadows, slithering up to the other guard before quickly and efficiently taking her down. Vanessa came out from where she had been hiding and walked up to us. As there were no cameras we didn't have to worry about anyone coming to check this place out or try and kill us.

In quick succession, two shots rang out in my ears and my hearing became muffled. My eyes, which were once accustomed to the dark, were blinded for a split second before they acclimatised again. Everything was playing out exactly like I had planned.

Flash Back

"Lucy, break in and cause a lot of damage. I will run outside and draw Ana towards me." Now pointing at one of the places in the woods I spoke again. *"I will be in here and you will be in a spot with a clear line of sight into the window."*

"So, I have to take the shot in that darkness?" Lucy asked, seeming to be scared. "What if I miss? What if I don't take the shot in time? What if i-"

"Lucy!" I said, grabbing her flailing arms so that she would stop and look at me. "I trust you."

She looked into my eyes, her worry very evident on her face. I wasn't sure that was going to change anytime soon but I needed at least to be confident in her shooting ability for just one day. The rush she would get after completing a mission and being one of the big parts of it would spur her on.

"Okay..." She said, but more like she was hyping herself up rather than answering me "Okay."

Present Day

I truly did trust her and it seemed my unwavering faith that she would make the shot on target was repaid.

Ana dropped to the ground, blood pooling in the clothes at her stomach. It seemed like the bullet had gone right through her, dealing massive amounts of internal damage. She tried pressing her hand over the wound and calling for help but as she did a plethora of blood shot out of her mouth. Quickly moving towards her I felt a massive amount of satisfaction as she looked up at me, with her dying eyes, in pure hatred. Relishing in the feeling that the person who hurt all of those girls was finally being put where she belonged, I realised that I wanted to be the one to kill her. I didn't want Lucy to take that burden on herself because even if she was a bad person, killing was something that most couldn't handle. Fishing my dagger out from its sheath I kneeled down to her level, flashed an open smile, before plunging the knife through her neck, forever ridding the world of her malevolent actions.

Our full plan was firstly for Adam to loop the security footage from the cameras in certain places. This allowed me to be the only one spotted, leaving Drew and Vanessa a clear run to get and release Isabella. Not only would they be free to release Isabella but also have license to roam the facility, taking out all the handlers so that the whole place was cleared of the horrible people that ran it.

I then drew all the attention of everyone inside the facility, including Ana, who would be too enraged by me popping up again that she wouldn't wait around inside, but would instead come out straight away, leaving behind all the newly trained assassins and the trainers looking after them, making sure they didn't escape. This left her open for an attack, which we were able to exploit because of Lucy. She did her job perfectly. Sitting by the tree line, she shot Ana just before Ana put a bullet in my head. As she lost control of her body her twisting fingers squeezed the trigger, firing a shot. Thankfully, it shot off into the sky and all was safe. I stood up, hearing the Academy's assassins-in-training coming towards me. They must have heard the shot. Bursting through the door, they froze once they saw the corpse of Ana laid out on the ground. They had all been under her orders and ended up seeing her as some invincible monster. Now that she was dead, they didn't seem to know what to do with themselves.

"Ana is dead." I said, trying to take control of this situation. All the young women looked up in response, appearing to have just seen me for the first time. "I am Katie, one of the assassins from the Academy."

A few had finally shown recognition of who I was. To them, I was just one of them... that was, until I had suddenly disappeared.

All of the previous girls who were no longer around had been executed in public, so I wasn't sure what they thought had happened to me.

"Y-you're alive...?" One of the girls was finally able to get it out.

"Yes, I survived." I answered casually. "In fact, I escaped the facility a few weeks ago."

My words caused a reaction like waves through the ocean, the shock appearing on their faces in an orderly manner.

"How did you get out!" A different, more confident girl asked me.

"During a mission, I slipped out with my partner." I replied, smiling. It was always nice seeing the ones who hadn't lost their spirit inside that dreadful place. By the looks of it a large majority from this group had. "You're now free to go."

Most stayed exactly where they were, the stark reality still not real enough for their fear-driven senses to take me seriously.

"We are going to give you money and the means to get wherever you need to get back to." I said. "We're also going to save everyone inside and help them get back home too."

The girls kept glancing at each other, in a daze, before one of them was able to stammer out an answer. "Are you s-serious?"

"Of course." I said, very serious. "This isn't the kind of thing I would joke about." Us

Finally ready to believe me, everyone started hugging each other and I could physically see tension begin to leave their bodies. Some started laughing while a few had silent tears rolling down their cheeks.

From the window I head footsteps. Judging from the direction, it had to be Lucy.

"Hey," Lucy said, sticking her head through the open window. She glanced over and looked towards all the other girls, deducing who they were and instantly concluding they weren't a threat by their behaviour. "I killed her, right?"

"You shot her and stopped her from killing me, but I finished her off." What I was saying was technically true since I did finish her off, but what I wasn't going to tell her was that she would've died anyway, even if I didn't intervene.

"Have you seen Vanessa or Drew since they went in?" She asked anxiously.

"Don't worry, they'll bring Isabella back. Have faith in them."

CHAPTER 11

Vanessa

Watching Drew fight all those guards made me question if I even knew the slight basics about fighting. I didn't show it but I felt as if I was more of a burden than a help. Drew had reassured me that what I was thinking wasn't the case. I don't know how she knew what I was thinking, but it still didn't sit fully right with me. Her graceful movements when taking down one person after another, while I was still really struggling with one, was what really made me feel inadequate. Even more so when Drew ended up taking them out instantly too. Drew had told me that the instructors weren't up to par with most of the students who had been there for over a year as they were brought in more for their knowledge than their actual fighting ability. This only made me feel worse, but I couldn't let it distract me, otherwise I would become an even bigger burden on Drew. Because of her, clearing the facility was going really quickly and we were almost done only thirty minutes into it.

"Where would Isabella's cell be?" I asked Drew, wanting to have more of an idea of where we both were trying to get to.

"Considering that she was a first year," Drew said, pausing, lost in her thoughts, "She'll be on the first floor at the back of the building."

Whilst we were both distracted, one of the trainers snuck up on me and Drew.

Or so I thought. Instantly, as if she knew they were there already, Drew ducked under the hand that held the knife in a flash, twisting her own into the neck of her opponent.

This was all done before I could even react. Done before I had even registered that there was a person sneaking up on us. I definitely did get jealous of Drew and her fighting prowess. The Feeling inferior was something I hadn't experienced in the past and was not something that I wanted to experience in the future either, but this time I was forever thankful to have someone as skilled as Drew on my side.

I had watched Drew in action so while what she did seemed very impressive, I wasn't able to fully gauge how much of a ruthless, excellent fighter she was. It was only when I fought against Katie and saw the massive disparity in our levels of skill did I finally understand how great they both were. With Drew, her body type, the oppressive feeling that she gave off, and her demeanour, reminded me of fighters I saw in movies. So, her being an amazing fighter didn't surprise me at all. What did surprise me was Katie, who didn't have any of the same attributes as Drew. In fact, the aura that she gave off was completely normal, like any random person. But she wasn't normal at all. Her fighting skills were only a little below Drew's and she had told me that she had been training for under a year while Drew had been training for more than a year. This wasn't just practice. The innate ability to learn that quickly, retain the information and be able to replicate it at a later date were all things that required massive amounts of hard work. Hard work that most people weren't willing to put in.

"Should we leave now?" Drew said casually, as if she hadn't just had a person sneak up on her and attempt to take her life.

Only once she had spoken did I release the breath that I hadn't realised I was holding.

"Yeah..." I let out. "...Let's go."

Drew sprinted on ahead, slowing down a little bit for me but I still had to run as fast as my body would allow me to keep up with her. Deep breaths calmed my heart, which was shocked to no end by the instructor who had managed to sneak up on us, as we ran to the back of the building. I glanced up and saw one of the cameras, making me wish that we had some way of communicating with the others so that they could tell us if anything was wrong, but alas, we could only keep our faith in them and make sure everything ran smoothly on our side.

Finally, at the back, we opened all the doors, trying to find where Isabella was being held. All the doors held girls, but it wasn't until two doors before the last one that we finally found her. She was curled up in her bed, to all appearances, asleep. Although, I could tell that she was only faking it, hoping that the person at the door would just leave her alone.

"You deal with her," Drew said, pushing me towards Isabella and backing off. "I'll be back in a few."

Drew ran off down the hallway and I did just what she said and dealt with the situation.

"Isabella." I said casually. "It's me, Vanessa."

She didn't turn around, only clutching the cover more tightly around herself. She obviously didn't believe me but all I needed to do to convince her was for her to see me.

"Isabella." I walked closer to her and then yanked the covers off, causing her to turn over wide-eyed.

It was at that exact moment that I saw the recognition register on her face and she leaped up off the bed, jumping at me.

"Vanessa!" She said, burying her face into my neck. I didn't feel tears but I knew that she was close.

I hugged her back for what felt like hours, glad that we had her back. While I hadn't spent much time with Isabella before she was taken, we were friends, and she knew that I was very good friends with Lucy, so she trusted me totally from the first time I saw her. They were sisters for a reason. Pulling away, I checked her over to make sure that there were no blatant injuries that needed dealing with urgently. Once I was satisfied with my visual search, I looked up at her face and saw her eyes shining.

"Lucy?" She asked in a small voice.

"She's waiting outside for you." I said softly.

A small, but genuine smile bloomed on her face. The look of pure happiness melted my heart.

"Is she okay?" Drew asked as she came through the door.

"Let's go then." She said once I answered that everything was fine.

I took Isabella's hand and we followed behind Drew, who was going a lot slower to accommodate both of us. It wasn't long before Drew took us out of the building entirely.

CHAPTER 12

Katie

Lucy and I took all the girls with us back to the car, surprising Adam.

"Who are they?!" Adam asked, clearly perplexed.

"New years." I answered.

"New year's?" Adam said, clearly more confused than before.

"The new recruits to the Academy from this year." I said.

"Oh...hi?" Adam said uncertainly, giving a little wave to the girls.

A few of them gave small waves back but most ignored him, focusing on being on the outside for the first time in a long time. They wouldn't have gone on any mission as yet so they had spent the months inside with no sun light and no air from outside. When they were hunting me down because of orders from Ana, they didn't have any time or brain capacity left to appreciate being in the outdoors. They probably never even realised that they were outside until they saw Ana's dead body.

"You not seen Drew, Katie or Isabella yet?" I asked Adam privately.

"I haven't heard from them but I still have control over the cameras and they're coming towards the exit. All three of them." Adam said while typing on his keyboard.

"Thanks." I said lightly, before walking over to the ever-nervous Lucy, who was getting even more timorous by the minute.

"Have you heard anything? Are they safe? Did Adam see them? Is Isabella ev-"

"Lucy!" I said forcefully, breaking her anxious ramblings. "Adam saw them coming towards the exit. They're fine."

She ran out of steam as soon as I got the words out, looking more embarrassed than nervous when I had finished.

"Oh..." She trailed off, clearly wanting the conversation to move in a different direction.

I spared her by smiling and walking away, moving towards the entrance to make sure that nobody was trying to escape or make it out safely from Drew and Vanessa's wrath.

After a few more minutes of waiting patiently Drew came out, closely followed by Vanessa and another girl, who must have been Isabella. Surprisingly, to me Isabella didn't look that bad considering how much time she had spent inside the Academy. She had done a good job staying out of anyone's way and keeping to herself. They had only been out a few seconds when a light brown and blue blur got past me and crashed into Isabella, nearly taking her feet out from under her.

"Isabel!" Lucy exclaimed, her voice thick with emotion.

"Lucy...Lucy!" Isabella's confusion and uncertainty made way for joy and exuberance instantly. "You're here!"

The two sisters hugged and cried, overjoyed at their reunion so long after having been parted.

I felt happy for Lucy. She had been the one to trust Drew and I straight away while Adam and Vanessa were hesitant.

She made the shot that saved my life, hitting her first target in such an important and stressful situation.

She really brought this whole mission together and allowed us to complete it. For that, I would be forever grateful to her.

Before I knew it, Lucy had come over to my side.

"Um, thank you for all the help," She said, looking into my eyes for the first time. "I'm glad that I met you."

Her sincerity was heart-warming and only made my respect for her increase.

"I'll be there if you ever need help again." I said with a small smile. "But let's hope that you never do."

"What are we going to do when we get back." Lucy asked me.

"Duh, a party, obviously." Adam replied, stopping me before I could speak.

I was thinking about rejecting that idea until I looked around at the faces of all my friends, clearly wanting to have a party. Well, except Drew, but when did it look like she wanted to do anything?

"What the hell." I said, sighing. "After we get these girls back on their way, we can have a party."

I ignored the cheer from the three before walking over to Drew.

"Did you take care of everyone?" I asked.

If we allowed even one person to escape then they could just make the same sort of facility and do the same sort of thing to other girls. We needed to be certain that no stragglers were able to get out and potentially come back for revenge in the future.

"I got everyone that I could see but I didn't get to check every corner." Drew said. "You can go back in and check. I'll keep watch over these guys out here."

I nodded at Drew and jogged off to enter the Academy again, this time though, of my own free will.

As I entered, a sense of nostalgia washed over me as I broke out in a cold sweat, suddenly feeling sick to my stomach as my memories were bombarded by all the hardships and pain I went through in here.

Walking along the main hallway, looking to check all the side rooms for anyone hiding, I came across the person who taught me how to first use daggers. She froze like a deer in headlights, before suddenly reacting, and tried to take me down quickly before I had time to react. Unluckily for her, I was already ready for her and easily sidestepped her attempt on my life before returning the favour and stabbing in and then out of her chest, in the region of her heart. I must have hit gold because she ceased moving, collapsing in a pile of her own blood a few seconds after. I wiped my knives off and put them back and carried on walking as I wanted to get out of this place as quickly as possible whilst still being meticulous, which wasn't the easiest thing to do I can tell you that.

Still checking the side rooms, I saw one filled with blood, rusty bloody tools and nothing else. A torture rooms.

As I stared into the room I suddenly couldn't get enough air into my lungs. A tingling feeling appeared in my fingers and my hands had started to tremble. Fear was crawling up my body and nothing I did was stopping it. I didn't realise what was going on until an image of Hugh flashed in my mind, putting me on the edge of losing control. I closed my eyes, trying to think happy thoughts, and took a few deep breaths. I continued this for a few minutes until I felt the panic start to subside. Not bothering with this room anymore I left it, continuing my search in the facility, wishing that what I had just experienced wasn't something I considered normal.

"Okay, and that's the last of them." I said, as we watched the last girl from the Academy walk off, a bag over her shoulder carrying all the things she needed to get back to wherever she wanted to go.

"I'm glad that's finally over." Drew said quietly. "Those girls can try and have a normal life now."

I pretended not to hear her and turned towards Adam, Vanessa, Lucy, and Isabella. Isabella was still riding the high of having her sister back and didn't seem to have taken in the fact that she had gone through a very traumatic experience that was going to stick with her for the rest of her life. It would hit her at some point in the future but, for now, she just wanted to enjoy the freedom that came with being able to do whatever one wanted to.

"Have you found a place to have it?" I asked Adam.

He had been looking for a place to have the party. Their old base wasn't in a good enough condition to host anything, let alone a party.

"One of my online friends offered the coordinates to a bunker that is in pretty decent shape." He said, turning the computer towards me so that I could see the pictures.

Although run down, the place was in much better shape than anything I had stayed in recently.

I nodded at Adam. "Good work."

He preened under my compliment, obviously pretty chuffed that he had found a place suitable for a small celebration.

A small smile escaped onto my face at his crazy antics and I shook my head. Adam was always able to lighten the mood and had been consistently doing it over the past few days, which I was really grateful for and appreciated a lot. He calmed down a lot of the girls before they left to start their new lives, making my job of explaining what we had given them a much easier task.

"So, are we leaving now?" Adam asked, looking like he was already ready to be at the bunker.

"Let me go and get Lucy and Isabella first," I said, looking over to where the two sisters were sitting. "And then we can go."

Lucy and Isabella had spent every second together since she had been saved. I let them have time by themselves to catch up as sisters and also so that they could help each other through their ordeals. I knew that not everyone was able to deal with coming out of the Academy in the same way that Drew and I were. Not everyone had the same thoughts, experiences, or temperament and so I needed to treat all these situations differently.

"Lucy, Isabella, we're leaving now." I called out to them, walking closer.

Once they finished talking, they stood up and walked towards me, stopping to ask a question.

"You found somewhere to go?" Lucy asked, curiously. "Where is it?"

"Well, Adam was the one that found it and it is a bunker that isn't that far away from where we are now." I answered.

Lucy's eyes suddenly became excited and she then turned towards Isabella grabbing both of her hands.

"This is going to be so much fun!" She said, her voice a pitch higher.

Isabella, who had looked quite nervous before, now looked as if she was calmed by her sister's excitement and was ready to have a good time.

It is," Isabella said, quietly, with a big smile. "It really is."

After close to an hour of driving we arrived at the sewer that held the entrance to the bunker. It took us a few days to get everything sorted and get into this position and I was ready for it all to be over. The walk was going to be long but that didn't matter to any of us. Because of this, plus the fact that the bunker was not close to any city or town, it wasn't surprising that no one had found it before Adam's online friend. Walking for a while, silence was the quotidian until we arrived at a door. It looked as if it had been bolted shut for years. No one would be able to open this if they didn't have the right tools.

"Uh, how are we going to open this?" Vanessa asked. "We didn't bring anything that can cut through metal, did we?"

I turned towards her and answered. "Lucy has her sniper, which still has the suppressor on it."

"Can you shoot it off?" I turned towards Lucy and asked.

"Yes." She answered.

Although her answer still lacked full confidence in herself it didn't mean that she hadn't improved majorly since just this morning. Taking out Ana and saving my life seemed to have boosted her confidence a little bit, but the real change happened once Isabella was saved. In the days since, Lucy was a lot more talkative, not only with her sister and us, but with others outside our little group as well. I only hoped that she didn't relapse back to where she was before we took out everyone at the Academy.

We all stood back and waited for Lucy to get ready. Once she had set up her gun she fired at the door, breaking the lock off with ease.

"Nice!" Adam said, being the first to react.

He rushed towards the door and opened it for all of us to see.

Inside looked a little worse than the pictures we had seen before but it wasn't anything major. Everything looked stable and we could stay in here for the night and until tomorrow.

As Drew and I stood at the entrance and looked around, Lucy, Isabella, Adam, and Vanessa got everything out and ready for us to spend the night. Food, drinks and unexpectedly, (well I guess it wasn't since it was Adam) he brought out a small compact speaker and started to play some music.

I was still standing in the entrance shocked by how much they had brought as I hadn't paid any attention when they went out to buy stuff or to what they were carrying in all the bags.

"Finally, everything is over!" Adam said, flopping down onto the floor looking relaxed.

I felt my gut drop at those words. Something didn't feel right at all, but I brushed it off as nothing. We had taken everyone out...right?

As I got more and more into the celebrations, a sense of warmth came over me, and as I looked around at all my friends having fun, I realised that I was so glad that me and Drew went to look for help on this mission. We really wouldn't have been able to get all of this done without them.

Just as I was about to tell everyone that it was too late to carry on, I heard a small noise which sounded like an explosion above me. I looked around but it seemed like no one else but Drew had heard it. Everyone was too distracted by their own antics that they weren't paying attention to their surroundings. I looked behind me and saw Lucy and Isabella standing there. Isabella looked confused but Lucy seemed to not realise anything was wrong. I quickly went over and turned off the music, causing everyone to look at me. I put my finger to my lips, signalling them to be quiet. They quietened down immediately and listened as well. After a few seconds, another rumble was heard from above, and then another and another. Each one getting louder. It was too late to get everyone out. All I could do was hope that no one got hurt by warning them.

"Bombs." I said, breaking the silence that had descended.

"What do we do?" Vanessa asked anxiously.

"Make sure you aren't under any of the collapsing part by the sounds that come down." I answered. "Now move, don't huddle u-"

I was cut off by the ceiling caving in and falling down on all of us.

I had woken up with a start; dazed and confused. That spell was broken when I saw all the rubble everywhere. I sat bolt upright, noticing how a large majority of the floor was covered in concrete and the ceiling was no longer intact, a semi-circle having been blown out of it. I thought back to before it had happened to try and remember if anyone was in the centre, but my mind was too muddled to do that right now. What I needed to do now was get up and search for everyone, because if one of them was injured, then they could be hurt long term if they were caught under any of this rubble.

Hoisting myself up into a standing position I started to carefully walk around, checking if anyone was under any of the rubble near me or on the ground around me.

Lucy and Isabella were the first ones I came across, seeming to be fine, with no debris on them, as if they had only passed out. Adam was fine too, although still unconscious, but Vanessa's lower half was stuck under some concrete. Using all my strength I could only get it to budge a little bit, so I needed another person to help me. Since everyone I had come across was passed out, I needed someone who would work well in this harrowing situation, and I figured Drew was my best bet. Just as I was about to leave Vanessa's side to look for Drew, I saw her walking around, looking like she was checking the ground for others too.

"Drew!" I shouted quietly across to her. We didn't know if the people who had done this were still here, or worse, were listening in on us right now. So being quiet was a necessity right now.

Her head snapped over towards me, scanning my body to make sure that no injuries were present. Once she arrived beside me, she was already satisfied that I didn't have any major injuries. She looked down to where I was pointing. Seeing who was underneath the fallen ceiling her eyes widened and she hurriedly got into a position to lift, only waiting on me.

"Come on!" She whispered. "We don't know how injured Vanessa could be under all of this."

I hurriedly scrambled to get into the same stance as her and we pulled with all our might. At first nothing happened, but as we pulled up even harder, it finally shifted. This then allowed us to move it out of the way so it no longer lay on Vanessa.

While Drew examined her lower body, I checked to make sure that her breathing was fine and that nothing had happened in her chest area: to her ribs and lungs.

Luckily, finding no injuries, I turned to Drew who was cradling one of Vanessa's feet on her lap. She had taken both shoes off which showed how swollen it was, proving that she sustain an injury. The one issue now was how bad was it?

"Is it a break?" I asked, citing the worst outcome first.

"It doesn't seem to be. Everything appears to be in the right place just from looking. I think it is a sprain, although I can't tell how severe it is or if my prognosis is even correct. Well, without special equipment anyway."

Inside the Academy we all got taught basic first aid knowledge but anything past that wasn't taught and was actively pursued against. This was because we were seen as disposable and anything more than mild sprains or other injuries to the body that were more serious would take too long to recover. It was quicker for them to just dispose of the injured person and bring someone undamaged in to fill their spot.

"Okay, good." I said, relieved. I trusted Drew's judgement on this, as always.

If it was anything above a sprain it would slow us down a lot as someone would have to carry her, and considering our group, the only ones fit to do that for long periods of time were me, Drew and Isabella. Adam was just a computer geek who never bothered, or cared, to train his body in any sort of manner and while Lucy did carry her sniper around a lot it wasn't as heavy as one might imagine. Especially when compared to an injured person.

Looking over to where Isabella and Lucy were, I saw that both of them were waking up, quickly followed by Adam, who jumped up instantly, hitting his head on one of the pieces of concrete sitting above his head.

"Ahhh!" Adam hissed, clutching his head. "Goddamnit!"

"Shh!" I said, showing to Adam to be quieter. We didn't want whoever bombed this place to hear us because Adam was shouting too loud. We wouldn't want this for any reason, but that really would be an idiotic way to go out, wouldn't it?

I shook my head at that thought and went over to Adam to make sure that he hadn't actually seriously injured himself from his little mishap. Once I got him to stop fidgeting, I checked his head and found nothing but a red mark where he had hit it. He didn't break the skin. Good.

There was a moment of complete silence once I had finished before Lucy blurted out what we were all thinking.

"Who did this?" She said, as if the words jumped right out of her trap and into the open. She covered her mouth, as if trying to reseal the door.

"Let's look around." I said to all of them, signalling Drew to stay by Vanessa in case she woke up soon.

Looking around the room was extremely hard. Dust was everywhere. Some of the concrete was in small pieces, littering the floor. Other pieces were huge and hung down from the roof, touching the floor, which meant that we weren't able to lift any of them.

"Found something!" Adam said, already walking his way back to Drew.

I noticed his treasured computer underneath his arm. Sighing, I brushed those thoughts away. At least he had found something, although it better be useful, I thought.

"What did you find?" Drew was the first one to ask him.

"This," He said proudly, showing us a piece of the rubble with a black logo on it, but then he unnecessarily continued. "It's a logo."

I internally rolled my eyes, glancing at the others who were doing it openly.

"Well duh," I replied. "What logo is it?"

The logo seemed generic in nature at first glance. If you didn't look closely you wouldn't be able to see what was within. It looked like a human with wings using a three-pronged trident to slay the helpless person beneath them who looked to have horns. The meaning was pretty obvious for all of us to see.

"I know." A voice said. Startled, I looked down to see Vanessa with her pained eyes open. "I know what it is."

We all stared at Vanessa, encouraging her to carry on.

"It is the brand of one of the most secretive, unknown and ruthless organisations." She paused to let out a cough and Drew gave her some water to clear her throat. "Nothing much is known about them. All I know about them is that they are probably the most well-hidden organisation that I've ever heard anything about. In fact, I didn't even think that they were real." Mumbling the last sentence, she left us all reeling.

If everything that Vanessa was telling us was true, it would mean that this definitely wasn't something accidental. As in, they were actually trying to, y'know, kill us, rather than them just blowing up an old unused bunker for the fun of it. That meant that we were a target and in their scope. Being that powerful meant that this wasn't the move to kill us. Thinking about it again, this was just a warning shot at all of us to let us know that they were here and ready for battle, although I still couldn't figure out why such a large ghostly organisation would want to target us specifically.

I'd have to look into it later on.

"Have they got a name?"

"I'm not sure if it is the real name of the organisation but I saw Kykl mentioned alongside the logo," She paused. "So that could be it..."

"Kykl? What the hell is that?" I asked impatiently.

"I don't know," she said, looking away from me. "I've told you everything I know."

"Sorry." I apologised, realising that I was taking my frustration over the situation out on her.

She nodded over at me and lay back down, obviously still in some pain.

"Let me search it up on my baby." Adam said, opening his cradled laptop and setting it down on his lap. He mumbled under his breath. "Can't let it touch the dirty floor."

I was going to retort that he was as dirty, if not dirtier than the floor, but I held off, realising that it wouldn't be a help in any shape or form. Adam started going through some weird avenues through the internet. The only thing I recognised him doing was opening a browser called Tor. Everything else went over my head so I just sat and watched, waiting until he was finished.

"Okay, so I'll check this chatroom first." Adam said, entering a site that contained a lot of text. This was all too much for me so I decided to check in with Drew and see how Vanessa was doing.

"I'm doing okay," Vanessa said in a livelier voice than just a few minutes ago. "Don't know if I can walk though."

Getting her out of here to the car would be a big problem. We were going to have to take turns letting her lean on each of us but considering how battered, bruised, and exhausted we all already were, having to support her was only going to make it harder, but we had to. We couldn't leave her behind even for a moment because the Kykl group could still be laying around somewhere and Vanessa wouldn't be able to run away if cornered.

Drew had checked to see if I was injured but I had never checked to see if she was. Walking up to her whilst looking for any obvious signs of injury, I asked Drew if she was hurt. She answered that she was fine but I wanted to be sure. Checking her thoroughly I only saw a few small cuts and everything else looked very normal and nothing was out of place. Taking her words on board, I backed off once I knew that she didn't have any injuries as far as I could see.

"I got it!" Adam said, his hands shooting into the air.

"What did you get?" Drew asked.

"People mentioning Kykl." He paused to lean in closer and started reading. "They are mentioned alongside an assassination organisation that takes in young girls and trains them up...oh..."

The organisation that attacked us right now was targeting us because we took down their precious Academy?

That was a massive shock to me. I hadn't suspected anything like that at all. That meant that Ana wasn't the one running the whole organisation like she presented. She was just a pawn to a bigger threat. That being the shady Kykl.

"Oh, shit!" Adam said, clicking around on his computer. "It's gone!"

"What's gone?" I asked quickly, noticing how frantically he was trying to spew his sentence.

"The post that mentions the two together is gone. They have been able to erase the account of the person who posted it. Their whole account is gone!"

"Is that hard?" I asked because I didn't know how much went into removing someone's comment from the deep web.

"Well, considering how the person that posted the comment actually had that information, which is very exclusive and unknown to almost everyone, we can deduce that they know what they're doing online in terms of security. This means that they have one VPN set up at least." He looked over to make sure we were still with him, which we were, before continuing. "So, there are three options. Either they got into his account within a few minutes - it usually takes me a couple of hours of trial and error - of him posting this comment while he had a VNP up, which means they're way better than anyone in the world. Or, they travelled to his location in real life to login into his computer and delete his whole account, which still means they're better than anyone in the world. Or..." He paused before carrying on. "...Or they are trying to bait us with information about them to lure us out."

Thinking about it, the last option was the most probable. Knowing how long it took Adam and how good he was, the other options just didn't seem realistic at all. The only realistic one was them bating us with real, genuine information about them. It didn't really matter if it was bait anyway because it was the only lead we had. The only way to end this was to follow the bait and try and sniff out their traps before we got caught in them.

"Hang on." Adam said a few minutes later. "I've just been messaging some of the people who were friends with the one who got their account deleted and they know where he lives. They said that even though he knew that information, not only did he not post it, but he was also keeping it on the low down. They also gave me his address because he doesn't want to risk using his internet again, in case they actually do something to him."

"They just gave out his address? Just like that?" Lucy asked, her eyebrows furrowing.

"It is because they know who I am and that I am trustworthy enough to be able to handle sensitive information like that." Adam said proudly, puffing up his chest.

"Okay..." Lucy said, still a bit perplexed as to why they so easily handed over private information, even if Adam was well known and trustworthy. How did they know that someone wasn't impersonating him?

Just as I saw that she was getting ready to ask him a question as she still wasn't satisfied, she closed her mouth again as Isabella whispered in her ear explaining why. After hearing whatever it was that Isabella had said, she seemed satisfied with the answer, no longer questioning.

"So where are we going?" Isabella asked, curiously.

"We are going to Norway!" Adam said eagerly. "I've always wanted to go there!"

Adam's excitement and announcement seemed to raise everyone's spirits.

"Are we going to go by plane?" Vanessa asked.

"Private plane specifically." I answered. "It is best if we don't let any strangers hold our lives in their hands, considering that we have Kykl trying to bait us and are obviously pretty pissed that we took one of their branches down."

Thinking about leaving this place was making me sad, which was the first time I had felt that in a long time. This place was where I had had the most fun in a long time. From getting kidnapped and being kept in a cell all day. Being forced to go through rigorous training all the time for months on end, every day, almost destroying my soul. On top of that, the stress from making sure that I made it out safely, that Drew made it out safely and my family weren't harmed or hurt at all, was a constant worry each and ever second I was trapped in that hell hole. Even simple things, like, when going to lunch we were persistently barraged by violence and killing, keeping everyone on edge and making them jittery. This made being able to have fun something that wasn't achievable to any of us during our torturous time there, even on the missions where we were away from most of that.

While some had it easy and were able to kill their target quickly and efficiently with nothing in the vein of repercussions or anything going even remotely wrong, I was different. With Hugh being murdered right in front of me, all hate I had shifted towards the others - not the Academy anymore, who had helped with my training and played on my want to be accepted so that I would do what they wanted.

Now that we knew that an elusive ghost organisation, that was way more secure compared to the Academy, was behind the Academy, it made me question whether they had actually sent me to that place and had Hugh there to be killed to "help me" discard my feelings of resentment that hadn't gone away from all the physical abuse and mental torment I had endured when I first arrived. The fact that it succeeded in doing that only reinforced my new thoughts on them being the ones responsible for the harrowing ordeal that I was unlucky enough to experience.

Maybe it wasn't just luck.

"We're leaving now." I said, disregarding my earlier thoughts and coming back to the present. I didn't want to wait here any longer as we would never know who was waiting for us or what they had planned if we did. "Who is going to carry Vanessa first?"

"It's fine." Vanessa said, hauling herself up using a piece of rubble that was next to her, while a pained grimace was etched on her face. "I can walk by myself."

She finished her sentence and then went to take a step forward. As soon as her good leg left the ground, she collapsed in pain, letting out an agonising hiss.

"This isn't the time to be proud." I said. "Let one of us help you."

Her face looked pained again, but this time it wasn't physical pain that scorned her. It was the mental anguish of feeling useless. Since Drew and I joined the team we had taken over her main role in the team, the first line, the one who did most of the physical work in the team. The fighter. Through our hard "training" we had been able to take steps that were incomparable to other regular people because of the harsh circumstances that we were put into. This wasn't something that Vanessa would want to experience, but the results definitely made her feel a bit inferior to us, although she really wasn't.

I would take being useless much more than Vanessa if everything that happened while inside that horrid place didn't happen to anyone ever again. With more help from Drew and I, she would progress in leaps and bounds in comparison to others who went through the same harsh experiences she had.

"Okay." She muttered begrudgingly.

Drew was the one to decide that it should be her carrying Vanessa and so we set off back to our car, while I took the lead, following my memory of how we got here in the first place. When we got back to our car, we weren't shocked to find what we found. Our car was no longer whole. It had been completely and utterly dismantled and destroyed. There was no chance that we were going to be able to drive out of here ever.

"Well, I guess we are walking." I said dejectedly, before carrying on past the car, glancing back to make sure that everyone was following me and were close behind. You never knew when someone might try to jump out on you.

I walked along the pavement, making myself adequately inconspicuous. You never wanted to seem like you were trying to go out of your way to disappear and make sure no one was watching you. That was a recipe for disaster, and also, I wanted the person I was following to notice that I was, which seemed to be working too. They ducked into an alley that was close by, their bodyguards, who they assumed I hadn't seen as they were trying to blend into the crowd followed, trying to keep out of my line of sight. I followed them into the alley and turned down the next turning where I heard footsteps coming from and saw the man staring back smugly surrounded by two guards.

"What do you want." He said sternly, obviously not viewing me as a threat anymore since I was a young girl. He kept glancing down at my body, like a complete creep.

"Oh, nothing," I said, pretending to be a bit panicked but, on the inside, I was sneering at how he looked at me.

"Why don't you come and do nothing with me." He said, licking his lips before looking at his bodyguards, which was obviously the signal for them to come and get me, but they didn't move from the position that they were in. "Hey! Didn't you see me giving you the signal?!"

He was complaining loudly when the bodies of his two bodyguards fell to the floor, blood pooling from the back of their heads. Leaving him all alone

"W-what happened?" He managed to get out, violently stuttering.

"Oh, I thought you wanted to do nothing with me," I said, my panicked face vanishing as I stood up straight with confidence. "We are making you nothing."

As soon as I said that I rushed him, leaving his fear-stricken body no time to catch up to his mind, which was just about to let out an ear-piercing scream. We can't be having that, I thought before slitting his throat, making sure that no sound was able to come out of his trap, before his body crumpled to the ground next to his bodyguards.,

I put my hand up to my ear and pressed the headset as Drew and Isabella melted out of the shadows.

"Have you got the rest of the family?" I asked through the headpiece.

"Yeah," Vanessa's voice rang back through my ear. Vanessa was still struggling a bit with her leg, but it had mostly gone back to normal in the weeks since and wasn't enough to stop her taking out a few people with no prior knowledge of fighting, indicating that Drew's diagnosis was accurate the first time.

Our plan was simple. Getting a private jet from some rich family by taking their identities and flying out to our destination of Norway, which wouldn't take long to fly to. Vanessa had knocked out the rest of the family, unlike me killing their dad. The only reason that I even ended up doing that was because I heard how much of an awful person he was. Added to the long list recently was leaving his wife and kids at home with no sort of protection, making this opportunity impossible to miss for us as we were in vital need of the resources that they possessed.

"Let's go then," I said to Drew and Isabella as we retrieved everything we needed before walking away, leaving no trace that we were even there, apart from the meticulously and precisely killed man and his bodyguards for someone else to find at a later date.

Although Isabella was still lacking somewhat in her knowledge of how to disappear without a trace after taking someone's life, we also used this to improve her skills so that we could better utilise her for any of our plans. It added more bodies to our arsenal that we could potentially need so it couldn't hurt anyone, except our victims.

We quickly arrived at the airport. Not seeing anything suspicious we got through everything quite rapidly. The people hired to fly this plane didn't know what the family looked like so when we arrived there and dismissed everyone, they didn't ask questions as they had already got paid in full. Drew went the opposite way from the rest of the group and into the cockpit of the plane. I followed, wanting to see what she said and what buttons and controls she used to take off so that I wouldn't have to rely on her only to do this kind of job. I would be able to do it too. Watching and listening to what she was doing did give me a bit of insight and as I was able to understand why some of it was done I would definitely be able to remember that, but the rest of it was too much for me to remember at one time so I left her alone. She needed to focus on this first and most important step. taking off.

I sat down in one of the seats and closed my eyes, not intending to go to sleep, but intending to get as much rest as possible during this short flight. I opened my eyes and looked towards her with enquiring eyes.

"Kaite?" Lucy asked from beside me.

"What do we do if we all get separated?"

"Why are you asking that?" I answered her question with another question.

"Since Vanessa's injury, I've been wondering how we would've coped if the injury had been more serious because she would've had to stay back on her own throughout the whole process of getting the plane that we're flying in right now.

What she was saying made complete sense and was something I hadn't really given much thought to. I contemplated on how to answer for a bit, trying to come up with the most logical and best way to deal with this situation.

"Hmmm, if we're separated here it will all depend on what kind of information we have at that time." I finally answered back. "We will always carry on with the mission so if someone is separated, as long as we know that they can take care of themselves, then we can all just go to the destination that we originally set out to arrive at."

She nodded at me, thinking my answer through before being fully satisfied and flashing a small smile at me. She then left my side, walking back to where she had been sitting with her sister and sat down again. I once more closed my eyes and rested until the plane had landed.

When we arrived and touched down on the ground, we tried to remain as inconspicuous as possible, keeping a watchful eye on all the people around us to see if anyone from Kykl was keeping tabs on the airports here, knowing that we would be travelling to the house of the guy they tried to bait us with.

Noticing someone that stood out just a tad too much, I tapped Drew on her shoulder and indicated for her to look at the man that I was seeing, just to reinforce my suspicions. Funnily enough, the first thing that stood out about him was the fact that he looked very normal. Almost a little too normal. Secondly, he was sitting down in the airport reading a newspaper, glancing up every once in a while, which would've been fine if he hadn't been sitting in departures - so he couldn't have been waiting for someone to come off a plane. Thirdly and lastly was something I probably wouldn't have noticed even a few weeks earlier. Behind his natural and calm expression was a hint of malice. A hint of bloodlust. A normal person would've had no experience with what that looked like, but I did. Most of us in the group did. I indicated to Drew to split up the rest of the team, leaving me with Lucy and Isabella. Lucy was helping to show on the outside that we were defenceless people that should be looked down upon in any confrontation

Like someone from a ghostly organisation would, he quickly noticed us once I moved a bit away from the crowd and acted like I was having a serious talk with the two girls with me. I was trying to draw him to us so that we could lead him into our trap that Drew was setting up at this very moment. He had noticed us and that was too bad for him as his life was already over. I had thought about taking out the earpiece for this trip as we were on a plane and I knew we would be next to each other the whole time, but now I was glad I hadn't been as Drew could give directions of where she wanted us to go and where the trap was set. Now, we didn't have to struggle with this guy.

I, along with the other two girls, began to lead the man outside of the airport, checking behind us to make sure that he was still following, using shop windows to pose and laugh, but all the while actually looking right at a Kykl spy. When we finally got outside the airport we walked leisurely towards a back alley, as if we had not a care in the world. No sooner had we entered the alley when the man rushed up to us, aiming to take us out. I felt pity for this person who thought that they were going to be living another day. I felt Drew's faint presence behind me and once he was on top of me, I dodged his attacks, throwing him off guard. When he turned around to have another go, Drew's arm slithered quickly around his neck, snapping it before he could make any sort of movement to react. With that one move, the whole situation was over. We no longer had to worry about this one-piece of the puzzle that was Kykl. "Leave the guy here," I said to everyone. "They'll cover this up for us."

They nodded back at me in understanding and we left the alley, taking a car to get closer to the location where we would find the guy from the dark web. We had done a bit of research before boarding the plane. Well, I say us, but it was just Adam doing what he does best and he found out that close to his house, there was a rundown abandoned building that no one entered as they feared it was haunted. Of course, it wasn't, but that didn't stop the superstitious locals from freaking out everyone else in the area so we decided to stay there as it was out of the way, no one would expect that so many people would be staying in a small house with no necessities and we could just pretend to be the ghost if anyone came by. It was a solution where everyone benefitted no matter how you saw it.

We had dropped off the essentials we had brought for the mission and since we had arrived in the middle of the day, we thought it would be the best time to get going to our only leads house. Splitting up into groups of two and not walking down the street as a massive group in this small town would draw less attention to ourselves. Another good thing was that all the houses were so far away from each other, leaving not much room to be spotted.

"Guys," Adam said. "That friend that gave me this address said that he only told the guy that we were coming today."

"Only today?" Vanessa said, incredulously. "Doesn't that mean that we are arriving unexpectedly?"

"We don't have time to worry about things like that if we want   to   survive,"   Lucy   said. They all understood that perfectly well after thinking for a second, and before we knew it, we were in front of this guy's house, arriving in our groups one by one.

I knocked on the door and a dishevelled man opened it for us,   smiling   widely. "Heyyy!" he said, seeming as if he hadn't slept all night. "You   must   be   Adam   and   his   friends!" His excited nature was more deranged than reassuring, but since we had numbers on our side, I wasn't worried about him trying on anything.

"Here, let me give you this first." He shoved a piece of paper into my hand quickly before turning around again and rushing off. "Come, come, follow me."

I unfolded the piece of paper and checked its contents, seeing an address written on the inside. I handed it to Drew to see if she knew what the address pertained to but she was just as clueless on that subject matter as I was. When we entered his computer room, I thought that his computers were off, but it was just the glare from the sunlight outside.

Angrily storming over to the curtains, he checked outside, making   sure   no   one   was   looking   in.

"So, what is this piece of paper and what does this address mean?" I asked him, making him pause in his actions.

"Ahh," He turned to face me, still having a tight hold on the curtains that he had not yet shut. "This is the address to a house that I found of the person who used my account to post that informati-"

His explanation was cut off by a loud bang that rang out through   the   house. First, there was deadly silence, but as soon as our informant dropped to the floor, a pool of blood quickly accumulating beneath the open wound on his head, everyone scrambled to move quickly into cover. And it wasn't a second too soon as continuous shots rang out throughout the house, destroying it.

As I was closest to Isabella and Lucy, I grabbed each of them and dragged them out of the back door. Drew, Vanessa, and Adam weren't as lucky because their position didn't allow them to escape from the same door as us so they had to go out the opposite door, leaving us separated.

We kept on running, leaving the house and all those who were trying to hurt us in the far distance. Anyone shooting from the place wouldn't be able to hit us from this far out as the distance was now just too great. I was able to completely and utterly book it as fast as possible and leave my friends behind in that sticky situation because I trusted them completely. Drew would be able to get them out of there safely with a bit of help from Adam and a little more from Vanessa. There weren't any doubts in my mind that we were all going to make it through today without losing anyone from our group.

It wasn't until we were a few more hundred meters away from the house, near the end of this small rural town that we started to slow into a fast walk.

"Was that them?" Isabella asked. "Was that Kykl?"

Although I couldn't be sure that it was them, I was relatively sure based on the fact that they only fired once we were all inside the house, which indicated that this assassination wasn't just for the guy we met with, whose name I still wasn't sure of, but was also for us because the bullets kept coming at the house after they got a clean uninterrupted headshot that instantly killed their first target.

"I can't be sure," I answered back. "But with how it panned out, it is looking as if that is the case."

"What about Adam, Vanessa, and Drew?" Lucy asked.

"I trust them completely to make it out of this situation without any major harm," I said, trying to sate her worries. "They've all got the experience and have gone on a lot of missions combined. If we were able to get away, they would also be able to do it."

"Yeah, I guess you're right." She said nervously, still obviously worrying about the other half of the teams' conundrum.

"Right now, all we can do is follow up on the address that was given to us by the internet guy," I said, taking the piece of paper out of my pocket. "I had already let Drew see what was contained on the piece of paper and her memory is much better than mine so she has already memorised it and will be trying to head there with Adam and Vanessa."

"So are we heading over to that address as well?" Isabella asked   me.
"Yes, we are," I answered back. "Drew already knows that we are always going to follow the mission and just trust in each other that we are able to accomplish the task that we are aiming for."

"Where is the location on the paper? Do you know?" Isabella   asked   next.
"It says here that it is in a part of the city that, from what I remember when I was researching Norway, is only about an hour's walk from where we are now," I said, thoroughly looking over the paper and trying to remember all my previous research. "Let's start walking now. We don't want to leave the rest of the guys waiting for us to appear."

We started the relatively short walk once I had determined which direction we needed to travel.

"How did you know how close we were to the area that the note listed? And how did you know which direction it was in?" Isabella, who was curious along the way, asked me more questions.

"I just did a little bit of research before we arrived here," I answered back. "I memorised the surrounding few miles and what direction each of the towns that surrounded it were in. So, it wasn't much."

Isabella and Lucy both looked at me weirdly, as if what I was saying wasn't a normal thing.

"Isn't that...normal?" I asked hesitantly.

"Bloody hell," Isabella said with a laugh that startled me. "No way is that a normal thing to do."

I contemplated her words and compared them to my time before joining the Academy.

What shocked me was how different researching things and retaining that information was compared to what I did now. It used to be so hard, but now I was able to do it like it was the most normal thing in the world and I didn't even realise when that change had occurred. It felt as if I had always been able to remember things this well when that just wasn't the case. Compared to my memory from before, which was classed as good against most of the people at my school, what I had now was like the contrast between night and day. It was exponentially different.

"And you do that for every place that we go to?" Lucy asked me, admiration clear in her voice.

"Yeah," I replied to her. "We can't seriously leave everything up to chance, can we?"

Lucy's look was full of awe and there was a hint of longing in her eyes. She was probably wishing that she had that kind of memory and was able to remember things under all the pressure that was constantly weighing down upon us, but what she didn't know was that the type of brain training that I did to get to where I was now wasn't pleasant at all. I would much rather have a bad memory than go through the torturous training that this type of memory required while locked up inside the Academy.

"Well, we are now close by so let's be quieter in case there are people standing guard." I said, once I recognised one of the signs indicating that we were only a few minutes away from the town.

They both nodded at me when I glanced back and we moved off the main road to the side so that we were a lot more hidden. Soon enough, we arrived at the location of the house and encountered no one. There were signs that people had been around the place so we had to maintain our stealth, but we came across the house and hadn't seen even a hint of an actual person still being around right now. Even inside the house, there was no movement.

"Wait" look over there!" Isabella said, whisper shouting and pointing to our left.

In the bushes, Drew, Vanessa and Adam were waiting.

Drew looked to be supporting Vanessa and Adam still somehow had a hold of his computer, which wasn't damaged in the slightest. Seeing as no one had come out and seen them and they were pretty easy to spot, I assumed that no one was around, at least anymore, and removed myself from the hiding spot, together with Isabella and Lucy, and walked over to the rest of the gang. They saw us coming over and I could see the visible relief on Drew's face. I thought it was for the fact that we were safe but as soon as Drew handed Vanessa over to Isabella and Lucy, as they were worried for her, the look of relief became more abundant.

Oh, she was just tired from having to carry Vanessa the whole time, I thought amusingly.

"It's good to see you safe and sound." Drew said.

"Of course, something like that isn't enough to stop us."

"So, are we going to enter?" Drew asked, questioning my intentions. "There doesn't seem to be anyone around."

"Yeah, let's enter now," I said to Drew before turning so the rest of the group could hear me. "We're going in now."

I decided to nominate myself as the person to enter the house first. Just because it looked abandoned didn't mean that someone wasn't still inside trying to make it look as if it was empty.

I pushed open the creaking door slowly, not to alert anyone of my presence.

The inside was as dilapidated as the outside but was a lot messier. It looked like someone had left this place in a rush.

Food was on the table that hadn't gone off yet, which was the biggest indicator that someone had been here very recently. There still seemed to be a few things that the person who had been living here had left, but none of the things that I could see seemed to have any value to our investigation into Kykl. There was also a router that was still plugged into a socket and the light was flashing on it. Adam would be able to look into the last time the router was used to see the exact date the person who had been previously staying here had last used it, giving us an idea of when they left the property. Through this, we could see what had caused them to leave and if it was us getting the information we got about Kykl, or if it was just a coincidence, which was highly unlikely. Once I realised that no one was inside, I called everyone in and got them to start opening all the draws and cupboards to see if there were any clues as to what this house had been used as or for.

"Found something," I said, causing everyone to come over to me.

"What is it?" Drew asked me, looking curiously at the book in my hand.

I flipped open the book to show all of them what I had found. Inside was a list of names with addresses and dates beside the names. The whole book was filled that way. No page was left clean. Some of the names had crosses through them, probably indicating that they had done what they needed with this person.

"A list of names..." Adam said, peeking over my shoulder. "What does it mean?"

"Probably a hit list." I said, as it was the only thing I could think of.

"Wait, no," Drew said, snatching the book from my hands and looking at the crossed-out names more closely. "This isn't a hit list. These are the names of all the girls who were taken to be trained for the Academy."

I quickly looked at the book again and saw a few names that I recognised from my time at the Academy.

"Stop!" I shouted, as Drew flipped through the pages. "Go back a few."

Drew flipped back through the pages until she came across what I was looking for and her face also filled with shock. My name was in this book and had been crossed off. The address was correct too, meaning that I wasn't mistaking it with another person who only shared the same name as me.

But that wasn't the scariest part about all this.

No.

The date beside my name was from years ago. From when I was ten years old. They had been watching me since I was ten years old and I never realised that anything was wrong at all.

The thought of them watching me from all that time ago sent a chilling shiver through every fibre of my being. This meant that they knew everything about me. Everything I did during those years had been watched and probably recorded somewhere else. I felt deeply violated by those thoughts, a sick feeling creeping up my throat. Next to the date there was a line, indicating that they hadn't stopped watching me, unlike some of the other people on these lists who had another date much later in time, indicating that they had stopped watching them at that time.

"Where did you find this book?" Isabella asked me.

I pointed towards a small chest of drawers that had three different compartments for storage. Drew went over to the drawer and opened the bottom one - one of the ones that I hadn't checked. There was nothing inside, well, to the normal eye anyway.

"Look," Drew said, pointing at the bottom of the drawer which was really close to the top of it. "A false bottom."

She dug her hands into the drawer and rummaged around, trying to find any leverage to pull up on, which she soon found. Pulling it up revealed another compartment beneath the main one. Only this one had things inside it unlike the last. A small book indented with the logo of Kykl, and a couple of other things that related to Kykl but the book was all our main focus.

Drew reached in and snatched the book from inside the draw, quickly opening it to see what was inside. Unlike the book that Drew had previously held, this book had writing next to the names, along with coordinates and addresses instead of just addresses. As Drew flicked through it, she froze on one of the pages, staring at one particular name. I didn't even understand what the book contained so I wasn't able to decipher why Drew was having this kind of reaction.

I indicated to the others to leave the room as I could see that Drew was being profoundly affected by whatever she was seeing. I took the book from her gently and looked at the same part she was looking at to see what it said.

Mary Ryan - Knew too much. Kept at...

And then some coordinates were listed.

"Drew, who is this person?" I asked, already having a horrible feeling that I knew who it was from her reaction.

"It's her," She said quietly. "It's my mum."

I was shocked. That meant this was a book about the parents of the children they had taken.

Drew had mentioned before how her mum was knocked out by the kidnappers at the Academy but that she never knew what had happened to her. Well, considering the date was fairly recent, only a few months old, we were in luck. The main question I still had was why they hadn't taken this book with them when they had left, and the only answer I could logically come up with was that they didn't realise that it was there. It must've been left behind by the person who was monitoring everyone before they were replaced.

"These coordinates. Let's look them up and see where she is." I said hurriedly.

Drew was broken from her stupor but still seemed to be in a little bit of a daze. "Yeah, let's do that."

When we exited, Drew allowed me to tell everyone what the book contained and why she reacted so strongly to it.

"Oh, we HAVE to find her." Lucy said, firmly. "Adam, look up the coordinates!"

"Already on it!"

Adam then looked up the lists of coordinates and as luck would have it, it looked like the place was very close by. Only a few miles from where we were.

"It's really not far at all," I said, looking at the map over Adam's shoulder. "Let's leave to get there now."

"Hang on, what about research on that place?" Vanessa asked.

"She's already done research on the whole surrounding area." Lucy said proudly. "No one else needs to do any."

"We'll only need to look more in-depth at the actual area and the place that Drew's mum is being kept in. The surrounding area I've got locked down."

Once I finished, everyone started discussing what kind of place they thought she was being kept in and Adam tried to look at the surrounding area.

Meanwhile, the one who was usually the most involved in these discussions was quietly sitting by herself, staring off into the distance, lost in thought.

"Hey," I said. "How are you holding up?"

"Y'know, I thought she was dead. All those years ago when I saw her in a pool of her own blood, I thought she wasn't alive any longer." She continued on very quietly. "I have mourned for her. I never thought that I might one day get the chance to see her ever again."

Her voice was raw and emotionally powerful. I felt the weight behind each word, and the meaning, and what lay below the surface. This was the second time I could remember since knowing Drew that she allowed herself be vulnerable in front of me. The only other time was when she was explaining the situation of her mother to me, and even then, it didn't feel like this.

"We will all help you find her." I said, putting a hand on her shoulder. "We aren't going to let this opportunity escape us. We will definitely succeed."

My words seemed to get to her and stop her worrying long enough for the clear thoughts to penetrate through and remind her of what it was that we were good at and what we could do. Those thoughts must have reassured her because after that, she didn't show her worry outwardly and was rational thinking, which allowed for less emotional thinking and more logical thinking. The help a lucid Drew would provide us with would be exemplary and wasn't something that we could afford to miss out on.

"Okay, I believe you." She said, her eyes showing full trust and commitment to whatever I had planned for this mission.

"First, we need to get there." I said, only now remembering that we hadn't moved from this dilapidated house yet.

"Okay, and what are we supposed to do now?" Adam asked once we arrived outside the facility that was said to be housing Drew's mum.

"First, we have to observe what they do outside the facility and how the whole operation functions." I said, carefully watching to make sure that every detail was entrenched in my head as the second part of the mission was going to be very tedious for me. "And then we have to have one of us find a way inside."

"One of us?!" Lucy asked worriedly. "Why just one person. Can't we all go inside?"

"Of course not," I said amusedly. "We would be much easier to spot and would get caught a lot quicker if everyone was to go in at the same time. If you're trying to sneak into a place like this, stealth is key."

Although, I wasn't sure sneaking in would be a possibility anyway. The amount of security personnel wasn't that staggering, but the type of mechanical security was state of the art. Plam reader, retina scanner and a voice manager were the second layer of security. The first being half a dozen well drilled guards, all with guns. Thinking about all the ways to get inside, I could only come up with one, which was something I really didn't want to try, but we may well not be given a choice to decide what we liked or wanted to do.

"Let's just wait until later and see if they do anything strange or if they carry on like this for a while," I said. "We can decide everything later."

While most of the less experienced people were getting distracted or not paying attention to the correct part of the facility at the right time, Lucy seemed like a seasoned veteran. She was intently staring at all the movement, as if they would move away and she would miss something if she were to even glace away for a second. That was the kind of determination that I loved to see. Her trying her hardest, even though she didn't have as much experience at this as anyone here, was commendable and only served to heighten her character in my eyes.

"Have you seen anything different from this morning?" I asked her, already knowing the answer to my own question.

She let out a sigh. "No, I haven't seen anything different since this morning."

"I guess we'll have to go with my first plan." I said under my breath before quietly calling everyone over to me and announcing that I had an idea on how to get one person inside.

"What is your idea?" Drew asked, suspiciously. "Because I didn't notice any change in the guards or their behaviour."

"I am going to get captured by them by acting as an innocent bystander and they'll have a guard take me inside to do whatever it is that they do to people they catch around here.

It was silent for a beat before protests swam around me, engulfing me and making me nervous that the guards may have been able to hear them, but luckily, when I glanced over, I saw nothing resembling a reaction so it meant we were safe for the time being. Well, at least until I had to enter that place.

"You want to go in alone?! That's so dangerous though! I'm not coming with you but someone else can!"

"I mean, you and Drew are the best fighters out of all of us, so it makes sense that it would only be you."

"But what if something happens to you...isn't there any other plan that we can follow...I don't want you to get hurt in there..."

"What if we knocked out one of the guards and had Drew go inside with you?

"No." I said definitively. "I am going in alone and that is final."

"Why isn't knocking a guard out and taking their outfit a good plan?" Vanessa asked.

"Look at what they have to do to enter." I pointed to the finger print scanner, the retina scanner, and the voice recogniser. "We can't get past that in such a short time through copying one of the guard's behaviour and hacking into that kind of system would take too long, right Adam?"

"Uhhh...I'm not sure that it is even possible to get into a system as sophisticated as that."

"That is why that wouldn't work." I paused for a split second to let that sink in before continuing. "And I can't take Drew in with me as I need her outside to coordinate the team if anything goes wrong. She is the only one with enough experience to do that."

"Couldn't you take one of us inside instead?" Isabella said, indicating herself and Vanessa. "We might not be much help but isn't that better than nothing?"

I shook my head sadly at her suggestion. It was good but it still wouldn't work.

"Look at the way the guards move around, the expressions on their faces and how they interact with each other. They are devoid of things such as sympathy and wouldn't go easy on you guys at all. I can take it. I have for a long time, but you guys haven't yet and if I can help it, I'll make sure that you never have to." I looked at their appearances, taking them into account and then carrying on. "The most innocent and harmless looking people here are Me, Lucy and Adam," There was some protest but I ignored it and carried on. "And the only one who knows how to fight out of all of us is me. While they might be ruthless people, they aren't going to inconvenience themselves by doing anything to the most harmless looking person as it would waste time." Looking around at their faces I knew I had got through to them and got them to see sense.

"How are you going to get inside then?" Drew asked me.

"I'll pretend to be a defenceless girl who has 'accidentally' stumbled across this place." I explained to them. "Then they'll take me inside because this is a sort of prison from what we've seen."

Drew nodded at my answer, understanding my thought process straight away and not finding a reason to question my action plan.

"Here, take all my weapons." I said, handing them over to Drew. "Right, I can get in safely now."

"Be careful." Lucy said, her worry reflected in everyone's eyes. The warm feelings from those looks didn't disappear as I put on the mask of a different girl and went out into the clearing, in full view of every one of the guards.

"Hey! What are you doing here?" One of them asked me, pulling his gun up and pointing it towards me.

"W-wait, what is this place..." I said, putting on a facade. "Where am I...?

With the confusion evident on my face, they let their guards down. Pathetic, I thought. Is this all it takes for these guards to not see me as a threat?

"You're coming with us." Two of the closest guards walked up to me and put their guns away, grabbing me by both of my arms and dragging me back towards the entrance to the Kykl facility.

"W-who are you, where are you taking me?!" While my head was frantically moving from side to side and I was flailing, inside my head I was smirking at the fact that my plan was going off without a hitch. "Let go!"

"If you don't want to get killed, shut the fuck up and follow us." His eyes threw daggers at me, although with my temperament it bounced straight off, which was something that he would never know. I obediently shut my mouth and stared ahead, wide eyed, noticing his glaring gaze change into one of satisfaction instead, making laughing a very appealing proposition for my brain. One which I luckily averted. I stayed quiet throughout the rest of the journey, acting passive and scared to make them let down their defences around me, but what I was really doing was observing the surroundings, trying to make a mental map for my inevitable escape. I was also looking out for any sign of Drew's mum as she was the reason I was inside this building in the first place.

"Get in and stay quiet!" One of the guards who was leading me along said harshly, pushing me inside a room and not caring about anything after. They walked away, leaving me alone in there with my own thoughts.

It was great that they didn't see me as any sort of threat and left me with no guards outside. With my performance having such an effect on their well-trained battle-hardened minds, an acting job might be on the cards. That thought kept me amused while I waited for any person to come over to me so I could observe and try and find Drew's mum as quickly as possible. We didn't have the time to stay in the same place for a long time as it would let Kykl have a much easier time catching us. It wasn't long before someone came to get me and take me, probably to see their superior.

"Who is this?" The person that I was taken to was an old, grey haired man and judging by his aura of invulnerability he was the leader of this place.

"She stumbled across this place."

"So, she saw too much? Put her with the crazy one."

I wasn't paying attention to their conversation until they started talking about moving me in with this person that was called the crazy one. Knowing these people, they weren't going to be crazy at all.

"Yes sir." As he lead me away I caught the hint of a frown on the boss before it vanished, as if it never existed.

I was thrown inside a dark cell, my eyes having to adjust quickly from the sudden change. As they did, I saw someone in the corner. I couldn't make any of their features out, except the fact that she was a woman, and I assumed that this was the lady who they referenced as, 'The Crazy One'. I decided to ignore her and leave her alone as she was mumbling in the corner. Words that I couldn't make out spewed from her lips, the sound being the same but the actual content wasn't legible unless I went closer, but considering the circumstances, there was no time to be wasted. I sat down on the bed farthest away from the other person and lay down, biding my time, as there was nothing that I was able to do in this exact moment. Or so I thought. The mumbling of the woman became clearer and clearer as my hearing got more and more attuned to the quiet. It was only after a few minutes of focusing on the silence that I realised what she was saying. I rushed over to her and touched her shoulder. She spun around and what I saw filled me with a joy I hadn't felt since I reunited with my own family.

In front of me was a red-haired woman. That alone wasn't enough to change anything in my heart but it was a combination of that, her face and what she was saying.

"Bring me my daughter. Bring me my Drew." The woman, who looked exactly like Drew, only older, said again and again.

"You're Drew's mother?" I asked the women, my voice wobbling.

Her unclear eyes suddenly had a clarity to them as she harshly grabbed me shoulders, the sudden intensity throwing me off for a second.

"What did you say?" Hope was clear in her eyes but a hesitant suspicion still showed. Probably from all the psychological torture they had inflicted on her since she was captured.

"Drew is your daughter?" I asked her, just making sure that I wasn't making any sort of mistake.

"You know my daughter? You know my Drew?"

"Well, I do know someone who looks exactly like you but younger, does that ring any bells?" I then asked her. "Drew Ryan?"

"That's her! It has to be her," She mumbled, before looking at me clearly again. "She was taken away from me when she was only a child and taken to the Academy. The people here always told me she was dead. She isn't dead?" Her rapid questioning was hard to follow but I did my best to answer, giving her all the information that related to her inquiries.

She let out a huge, relived sigh once I told her that her daughter was fine and not dead. "I'm so glad...so when am I going to see her?" She paused and then frowned. "Why are you in here instead of out there with her?"

"We read that you had been captured and kept inside this facility and we wanted to know what they meant when the book said that you knew too much." The look on her face let me know that she understood exactly what they were referencing. "Well, we can deal with that once we get out of here. It shouldn't be too hard from what I've seen with their security and personnel."

"So, when do we leave?" Her excitement over the mere thought of getting to see her daughter was bringing the fight and brightness back into her eyes. Something I was sure she hadn't had since the day she lost her daughter.

"Next time they open the cell we are going to get out. Leave all the fighting to me and just follow closely behind so that you can tell me if anyone comes up behind us at any time." I explained. "For now, just wait and act as if you are your normal self, I'll do that same."

She nodded her head firmly and turned back to her wall as I walked back to the bed and lay down. While she didn't mumble anymore, her mannerisms were the same as they were before clarity had taken a hold on her.

It was a few hours before we heard anything from outside - the sound of boots on a solid floor - which signalled and brought about my change into the unassuming, harmless girl that I had portrayed myself as.

"All right, get out now girl. You've spent enough time in here!" I walked up to him, using my scared facade to check all around and make sure that no one was close enough to hear. Once that was confirmed, I dropped all pretences and made sure that the last thing that guard remembered was my cold face staring back at him.

"Come on, let's go." Mary didn't seem to be that bothered by death and I can't say I was surprised, considering how long she had been inside this place.

I held up my hand indicating her to stop as I heard more slow footsteps coming towards the corner we were just about to go around. The guard didn't even register what was happening before I took him out with a quick blow to the back of his neck. I was having to do this unarmed which was making it a little harder, but I was still skilled enough to make it through this mission without any weapons. We encountered a few more guards along the way but because there were so many things in the hallways we could hide behind, it wasn't a problem to do that without getting caught.

"The exit is just over there." I said, running just in front of Mary, making sure to match her pace so she didn't get left behind.

Once we exited, I realised why there had been so many sounds. Drew, Vanessa, and Isabella were fighting some of the guards, whose guns were strewn across the floor far away from them, making the battle more even, even if they had larger numbers on their side.

Once I joined the fight, after leading Mary over to the others who weren't fighting, it was over and nobody was left alive.

"You good?" I asked the girls.

They all nodded once they had checked to make sure that everything was actually fine.

"Did yo-" Drew started, but I cut her off by pointing over to the side. To her mother.

Drew stared at her mother, quietly, not reacting. Mary, having the same reaction, was the first of the two to break from her apathy and slowly, in a dream-like haze, walked towards her daughter and touched her face delicately, as if she didn't believe that who was in front of her was real.

"Drew...?" Her shaky, quiet voice sobbed out of her. "Is it really you?"

While her mother's face was emotional - a mixture of sadness and happiness - Drew's was completely emotionless. The only hint that she was feeling anything was in her eyes.

Drew

The feeling of seeing a parent that you thought was dead for so long wasn't something that I was able to accurately describe. When Katie saw her mum again for the first time, I didn't understand her reaction at all, but now I did. I understood it fully. The mixture of happiness, sadness, and anger inside me culminated in confusion over what I was really feeling, contrasted with the emotional maturity that I lacked from my time inside the Academy. While the happiness and sadness were easily explainable to me, the anger was harder to justify. I knew that she didn't leave me. I was taken and it was out of her control but, it didn't make the animosity I held towards her less, which was not something I wanted to have. I wanted my reunion with my mum to be full of happiness and nothing else, except maybe a little bit of sadness mixed in, but this feeling was horrible and I was going to need to get rid of it soon. It was something that only Katie would understand. She would be able to help, I thought, calming myself down.

I stayed in my mother's arms for a while. Basking in the mixed emotions that were gradually taking me over. She pulled away after a short moment, seeming to sense my cluttered feelings, if her sad smile was anything to go by.

"Sorry to interrupt," Katie said from the side. "But we have to leave."

"Yeah ok-"

As I was replying, we heard the sound of more cars racing towards us at speed. More enemies were the only thought on my mind. I moved in front of my mother in preparation to protect her and we waited for them to come to us.

Katie

Around twenty more guards came out of the cars. Only this time they didn't have any guns and seemed to be more suited to quick, fast combat. They wore lighter vests that were a lot less padded and by their movements, seemed much less weighty.

I looked to my side and saw that Drew, Vanessa and Isabella had already lined up beside me and were ready to fight, leaving the less combat-experienced ones protected behind. We split up evenly and made sure that Drew and I took the brunt of the all-out assault as we were the best fighters here and also had the most experience. I nodded over to the girls standing by my side. And then we were off, stalking towards two guys who were doing the same to us.

The clash was brutal and hard work. Although I had a lot of experience fighting highly skilled people, I didn't have as much when fighting multiple people who knew how to fight, which made this a learning experience for me.

As Drew and I were the only ones with weapons, we finished quicker than both Vanessa and Isabella and decided to help then out, but when I looked over to Isabella's side to help, I noticed something really strange. It looked like she was holding back her movements to seem like she was worse at fighting than she was. She would go for one of them as if she was a skilled veteran but then, as if she remembered that she wasn't supposed to be showing her skills off, she retracted that and put in a lot less finesse and power into her movements, making her look more clumsy. I put that away in the back of my head, making sure to keep an extra eye on her from now on. The fight with all the guards was soon over and they were now dead or knocked out.

"Let's go now," I said, after we had checked all their bodies for any information on Kykl, but found nothing at all.

Everyone got into the car and we started to drive away. Remembering what Mary had mentioned about telling me the things I wanted to know, I decided to start questioning her.

"So, what is it that you were going to tell me before we got that chance to escape?" I asked Mary. "Will it help us taking Kykl down?"

"It will..." She replied, hesitant on her next words. "But there is something I wanted to tell Drew first, before all that. Something I'm sure she would want to hear."

"What is it?" Drew's cool voice answered back, although curiosity was clear on her face.

"It is about before you were born." Mary started. "Back when I used to work for Kykl..."

Through the trees, the grass, and the dead men carnage on the floor, through all that, there was something that no one noticed. Something that none in the party had registered that had been there the whole time. Someone who was watching all the interactions between the party of people trying to take down Kykl.

Standing there as if nothing was wrong was a grey-haired man. He had a small smirk on his face as he watched the car drive off into the distance.

"They are a little better than I thought." He let out a voiceless laugh while looking at the bodies that were strewn around the floor. "No matter, it'll all turn out the correct way in the end."

Those were the last words spoken before the old man walked off into the tree line and disappeared into the forest, not a whisp that he had been there left behind.

CHAPTER 13

"You used to work for Kykl?!" Out of all the things that I had expected her to say, this was the last on the list.

"Yes, before Drew was born, I used to work for them." She said. "Back then, they were a genuinely good company, which is why I even worked for them in the first place."

"I find that hard to believe." Vanessa mumbled, although all of us could hear. I shot her a look and she rolled her eyes. We were all thinking that but it didn't have to be said out loud.

"No, it's okay. Looking at how they are now I wouldn't have believed it if I hadn't worked for them back then."

"When they first started off, they were an organisation that was making a big difference in the world, positively so. It was on that high that they started to realise that doing these good deeds didn't pay the bills and they were actually starting to lose money." She sighed. "It was then that a very powerful few people offered to buy the company out. They offered to keep all the employees and vowed to make sure to keep the same kind of image, but have a side business to make some money so that they could run on their own. Everyone who worked there was ecstatic and the owner accepted their deal and everything was looking up."

"What happened next?" I asked, once I realised that she got lost in the past.

"Next...right, next. The company slowly started to disappear from the internet and the business coming their way started to slow down considerably, until one day, no one was looking towards them anymore and it was like they had never existed in the first place. Some of the employees went to speak to the new owners of the company but mysteriously disappeared and were never seen or heard from again by anyone who knew them, which, while not uncharacteristic to some, was completely out of character to the large majority. Still, at that moment, no one suspected that the new owners had anything to do with their disappearances."

"But they did, didn't they?" Drew interjected.

"They did. When I found out, I was already pregnant with you so I knew that I had to leave." Mary smiled at her sadly. "But once they found out that I was trying to leave they killed my husband. They killed your dad, Jack."

Drew was stone-faced throughout the whole conversation, but once she learned of the fate that beheld her father, I could tell by her slightly clenched fist that she was affected and wanted to kill everyone who had any sort of involvement in the murder of her dad.

"After that, I asked a few of the people who were unhappy with the company to help me escape while keeping them off my tail, which they did well, but which also ended up costing them their lives." The genuine anguish on her face and in her voice was enough to stir most of our hearts. All of us knew what it was like to lose people near and dear to us. The thought of losing so many at the same time wasn't explainable by words. The pain, the feeling of pure hatred, the agony and suffering that you had to go through every day because those people were no longer there wasn't something I would ever experience again if I could help it.

"They knew that I knew too much so they kept trying to track me down." She sighed wearily, looking out the window at the moving scenery. "And once they found out that I had a daughter, they were even more interested in me, wanting to take her as one of their assassins in the Academy. My worst nightmare came true and they, unfortunately, ended up succeeding. They also captured me so that I couldn't do anything to interfere with their future plans and to stop me trying to get Drew back."

The story was tragic and it really made me feel for her.

All the friends she'd made from her workplace were slowly killed off. Her husband, who wasn't involved in the company at all, was also killed by her employers. She was also kidnapped and taken to a facility where she stayed for years on end and if that wasn't bad enough, her daughter, who was only a few years old at the time, was ripped from her grasp. No wonder they called her the crazy one while locked inside that containment centre.

Did I do enough? Could I have done more? What would have happened if only I'd moved away a bit sooner? Would I still be by my daughter's side with her safe, sound, and innocent?

These were all questions that I was sure she had asked herself a million times now already - anyone would in her situation - although in the end, they were all pointless because life didn't care about what could've happened. All it cared about is the present and there was nothing anyone could do to change that.

"We are arriving now." Adam said from the driver's seat causing all of us to look out the window at our destination.

It was a small place, only a few hours away from the Kykl facility, but considering that everyone we had encountered was now dead at the previous place, we weren't going to have to worry about them informing anyone here. The dilapidated house was in the middle of nowhere, which gave us a lot of time to get ready and leave if anyone did try and take us down. At first, I had been surprised when Adam had told me he was the designated driver for all their missions, but once I realised that the other two options were Lucy and Vanessa, I fully understood why they had made that decision. Vanessa the hothead, would probably lose her cool in the middle of a mission with the subsequent road rage ruining everything. Meanwhile, Lucy was much too nervous. She'd probably draw too much attention to herself in the opposite way, by being too hesitant, compared to Vanessa. It was the most logical option to keep him as our driver for the foreseeable future. It would also give Drew the ability to help me with any fights while the others drove on, which was always a good thing.

"Let's go in," I said as the car stopped right next to the house.

"If you used to work for Kykl you must know where their base is located," I said, to Mary.

"Yes, in fact I do know where it is," She said. "It is back in England, close to London."

"That is really close to the Academy HQ..." I said under my breath, only now realising how close we had actually been to the main brunt of the enemy forces.

"What about other places?" I asked, wanting to make sure that if we were to take down this facility another one wouldn't pop up. "Are there any other people that could bud a new main HQ for Kykl?"

"Most of the people working for Kykl are only doing so because so much blackmail information is held on them. The people most affected are the rich and powerful because the poor people can't really be used for much except the odd job here and there." Her face lit up and her mouth opened as if she just remembered something. "Ah! Have you heard of someone called Ana? Ana Rodriguez?"

My heart jumped into my throat at the mention of that name and I looked at her strangely. How could she know about Ana while being trapped inside that containment facility for so long?

"I knew her when she was a little kid. I was nearly ten years older, but we were really good friends." Once she had finally looked at me her face froze. "You've...heard of her...right...?"

The hesitancy on her question was enough to make me pause for a split second, but I recovered and told her the truth.

"Yes," I said. "I knew Ana."

"Knew?"

"She is dead now. I killed her." I snarled, not trying sound too harsh, but was struggling to repress all the horrible memories trying to surface once her name was mentioned.

"Why would you do that?" The confusion was evident on her face, but the fact that she didn't look at me accusingly was enough indication that she knew there was more to the story.

"She was the one who was hands-on, running the whole Academy," I answered back bitterly.

What I told her seemed to be the most shocking thing of the night.

"Ana...was running the Academy...the one that Drew was in?"

"Yes," I sighed. "She had also been in the Academy when she was younger."

"What...?" She furrowed her eyebrows. "But she was such a good girl...why did they pick her and why did she turn out like that...?"

Her rhetorical question hung in the air, untouched.

"Come on now," Adam said, walking into the room and interrupting our conversation. "It's really close to leaving time."

I nodded at him and said bye to Drew's mother, giving her an awkward pat on the shoulder before walking out of the room. I still wasn't sure how to act around her.

Getting restless from all the startling revelations, I decided that a short walk, just around the house, would be enough for me to calm myself again, while also returning with a clearer head.

"What is it?" I asked gently, not stopping my walk but slowing down a bit as I felt the presence of someone very familiar behind me.

"It's... it's..."

"Is it about your mother?" I finally asked Drew as she arrived beside me.

"Yes." She said, letting out a sigh of relief that I had been able to see what she was trying to say. "It is about her."

I stayed silent, letting her sort out her thoughts on what she actually wanted to say compared to what she was feeling.

"It is just so hard." She burst out with, breaking the silence. "I want to be happy that she is here, but I don't know why I feel so much hate towards her. I know that she didn't leave me by choice, but that doesn't make the hate diminish at all. In fact, I think it makes it even worse."

Although I didn't have the same sort of feelings towards my family and couldn't understand where she was coming from, I could at least listen and give advice. It wasn't much, but maybe it was enough.

"There isn't anything you can really do expect build up another relationship and mention those grievances that you feel towards her."

She thought over my words as our loop finished and we came back around to the door

"Okay, I'll give that a try." However hesitant she was, as long as the idea was given a chance and she tried to change her view of her mother, I would be there and help her with it. "Thanks, Katie, I don't know what I would do without you."

It was now time to leave this small, abandoned house for England again. As usual, we found our way back by plane, because although Norway was at the coast and we could've taken a boat, it would take too long.

Something I hadn't thought about until we were on the plane was that Kykl were located in the same place as my family and friends. I had left them there to take down the Academy and make sure that no one could hurt them. And yet, I had left them in the clutches of a more powerful company that had done an unmentionable number of despicable things and the things that they were willing to do were much worse than the Academy would do. All I could do was hope that we arrived there in time to stop them from making a move on my family.

I looked over at Drew who was sitting next to her mum. She hadn't got around to telling her mother that she wanted to restart their relationship from scratch, so while her mum was trying to start a conversation with her, Drew was being short and awkward. This gave me a new thought. We weren't going to be able to take Drew's mother with us while trying to infiltrate Kykl because she didn't bring anything to the team. She would not only provide us with no skills that were helpful, as she only had information, she would also burden us because she would need protecting. That's it!

Mary could stay with my family. We passed there on the way to Kykl's HQ and I had wanted to check on them and make sure that everything was fine so it wasn't like we were wasting any time on this.

I was going to tell Mary immediately, but then I realised that it would be better to tell Drew first as that would relieve some of the shock and diminish the reaction she would have to my idea.

"Drew, come over here for a sec. I've got something to tell you," I said, indicating the seat next to me.

She looked over at me and nodded before telling her mum that she would be back soon.

"We can't take your mother with us when we go to Kykl."

"I know, I just don't know what we can do with her though."

"She can stay with my family," I said, watching for her reaction.

Drew looked up at me quickly, shocked at my words.

"But won't that put them in more danger?" She asked. "They know who my mother is and we know that they would put her inside of a prison, or worse, because of how damaging the information she has on them is."

"You're right that they won't want to leave her, but that is why we are going to finish the mission in as little time as possible, before they are able to send word out to go and search for our families."

Once she had thought over my words, she realised that I was right and agreed.

"You should tell her," I said, once we had finished.

"But it was your idea..." She trailed off, glancing nervously at her mother, who glanced over and gave a small smile.

"She is your mum; it will be best coming from you," I sighed exasperatedly before shooing her. "Go on."

Drew could fight a room full of trained operatives but struggled to talk to her own mother about, anything really. I watched over them as they talked and saw Mary very receptive to the news, talking about how she didn't want anyone to not have the ability to perform at their best. Once Drew was finished, Mary looked over at me and smiled gratefully. For giving her a place to stay out of trouble or for getting her daughter to interact with her more? I didn't know, but that didn't matter right now as we had started to descend.

Once touched down, we exited the airport and before we knew it, we were on the way to my house. As it wasn't far away it didn't take much time at all and before long nostalgia was gripping my stomach tightly as we drove through the streets that I had walked for the first sixteen years of my life. The excitement started bubbling up as I realised that I was going to get to see my mum and friends again for the second time in a while, which was what made the excitement even more intense.

Pulling up to my home, I got out of the car and just stared at my house. Looking at it after such a long, brutal time was akin to a therapy session. Nothing about the house screamed anything wrong so I instantly relaxed, but still held some hesitancy that something could happen. It wouldn't calm down completely until I actually saw that everything was alright with her. Deciding I had waited long enough, I walked up to the front and knocked on the door, the others following behind, hesitantly. When the door opened, world instantly brightened as my mother stared back at me, unblinking.

"Mum..." I said softly, as I basked in the feeling of seeing her again after such a long time.

"Katie!" She exclaimed, as soon as she realised who I was, a beaming smile plastering itself on her face. "Come in! And bring your friends with you."

I nodded at her and walked in, letting everyone know that it was okay to follow after me.

"Did you do it?" She asked, once I had settled down on the living room sofa. "Did you get rid of that place?"

I did. Well, only with the help of all my friends here." I scratched the back of my head. "But...something else came up."

"Are you going to have to leave again?" The happiness had vanished as soon as a hint of me leaving again came up.

"Not for as long as before. Only for a little while."

She let out a tired sigh and it was at that moment that I saw all the stress and worry I had caused her to come back and weigh down heavily on her. The guilt that suddenly hit me came in waves. I was making life harder for my mother. Someone that I wanted to have an easy life with no stress and worry. If I could stop this mission and have it completed by other people I would, but unfortunately, I didn't have the luxury and so I could only hope that she wouldn't have to worry for too much longer and that I could get back home to her.

"Oh, I forgot to introduce you to my new friends," I said, trying to change the subject. "This is Adam, Lucy, Vanessa, Isabella, and Mary."

"Hello, Katie's mother," Lucy said nervously, while Isabella gave a little wave and smile from beside her.

"Hey." Vanessa said casually.

"Hiya!" Adam said enthusiastically. "It is so great to meet you!"

"Hello," Mary said, giving a polite nod to my mum.

"Hello everyone." She replied back, the stress seeming to be a thing of the past. At least for now.

"I was wondering if we could stay here for the night and Mary could, maybe, stay here when we leave?" I wasn't sure what her answer would be, but I was pleasantly surprised when that seemed to relieve all the worry that had accumulated over the past few minutes of conversation.

"I would love it if you guys stayed the night," She smiled brightly, although there was some triumph behind it, as if she had planned everything to get me to stay. "And Mary can definitely stay here when you guys leave."

I felt so grateful to not only have a mother who was kind and caring but also understanding. A normal parent couldn't bear to see their kid go on such a danger-filled mission where death was a constant risk, but she supported me in my endeavours and it made the world of difference. Although she was constantly worried and definitely didn't want me going on this mission, she wasn't going to hold me back or let her parental instincts take over and she has allowed me (and still was) to do things only I can do, and accomplish things only I can accomplish.

"It's been a long day," She said to all of us. "Some of you might have to share some rooms but I've got guest beds and covers for everyone here if that's fine with you all?"

We all readily agreed, the fatigue from all those hard-fought days finally catching up to us.

I took my own room and Drew came with me. The others were split between two rooms.

Lucy, Adam, and Vanessa were together as that was something they were used to. Isabella was added into that equation because Lucy insisted, but judging by Isabella's face, she didn't mind at all.

Drew and I quietly got ready and slipped into bed and Drew was out like a light.

I stayed up, trying to process all the information that had been given to us by Drew's mother, Mary. After a while I got up as I needed the toilet.

Walking along the corridor to the bathroom I heard some talking but as it was probably just someone from the team, I left it alone and used the loo.

Walking back, I heard the same talking, but this time, I listened in to see what they were talking about, even though the woman's speech wasn't clear.

"...Kykl...I'll do my best...I won't let you down...Yes sir..."

Whoever was talking sounded as if they were talking to someone at Kykl! I quietly rushed down the stairs but because I hadn't been in my house for such a long time I had forgotten where the floorboards creaked and where they didn't. I heard a scrambling sound before the person who was inside the house was outside, the darkness masking whoever it was that had been talking on the phone. Making sure that no one else was downstairs, I then went upstairs and checked the rooms one by one. Vanessa, Isabella, Lucy, and Adam were sleeping soundly inside their rooms with no one visible anywhere. I didn't need to check the room Drew and I were staying in as I was in there only moments ago and Drew could handle herself perfectly fine even waking up from asleep. The only room left was my mum's. I opened the door quietly and let out a sigh of relief as I realised no one else was inside. That sigh quickly turned to suspicion when I realised that Mary wasn't in the room. Making sure that I wasn't missing where she was actually sleeping, I felt my blood start to grow cold. Could Mary be a secret Kykl agent sent to throw us off? No, that couldn't be the case. She had given us too much useful information. It just wasn't realistic.

I had walked out of my mother's room when I came across Mary, who jumped.

"You scared me." She said, her voice showing slight signs of trembling.

"Sorry." I apologised. "Where did you come from?"

"Ahh, I just went to the toilet a couple of minutes ago."

I nodded at her before wishing her goodnight. The direction that she came from was in the opposite direction to the stairs. There was no way that she was lying. Once I had finally convinced myself, I fell asleep, thoughts of who this person could've been swimming through my unconscious mind.

"Are you sure you've got everything you need?!"

"Yes mum, I'm sure. Look."

I was happy that my mother was fussing over me. I had missed that feeling. I could take care of myself but sometimes, having someone there to worry about you could make everything a little bit better. The pang of guilt from leaving her to worry again so soon after coming back did disrupt my mood, but the genuine care and affection that she was showing me melted that away and left me feeling deeply content.

"Okay, good." She let out a sigh, her hands clutched in front of her. "Good..."

"We'll be going now mum." I hugged her. "I'll see you when I get back."

She squeezed me and let go, waving goodbye as we entered the car.

"So where is this place again Isabella?" Adam asked, referencing the conversation that we had earlier on involving her.

This morning, Lucy and Isabella had been gone on their own for a while, which wasn't uncommon, but them coming to find me straight after they returned from whatever world they were in wasn't something I saw often at all.

"Isabella has something to say to you." Lucy had said.

Isabella then explained that she had heard some things that pertained the mission we were trying to undertake right now. Things that had to do with where the leaders of Kykl stayed, because of course they wouldn't want their positions compromised if the HQ of Kykl was destroyed. Or at least that was what Isabella could remember. She had seemed genuinely nervous, but there was something about her behaviour that threw me off. I wasn't sure what it was but it definitely wasn't something I would be able to figure out in such a short space of time.

Comparatively, Drew's mother, Mary, was someone who was extremely suspicious and what she had been doing in the night only made that more evident, but there was something about her personality that made me doubt it was her on the phone last night.

"I remember overhearing Ana talking about their cabins in the woods, a form of protection as they were so hard to find in the densely overgrown forest," Isabella said, Lucy and I on either side of her. "I saw a picture with markers of where the cabins are located and, because it was something that I had thought of as weird, I have remembered exactly what the map was about and what it said since then. Look here."

Isabella leaned over to me, pulling out her phone. We all had one but we just had to make sure that we didn't use it in any capacity that could allow potential malware onto it. After unlocking, her calls showed up for a split second, showing call to an unknown number that was a few minutes before I had heard the phone call from downstairs and that only lasted a few minutes. The timelines matched up. She was off that screen before I could see anything past the time of call and the duration, but she was a split second too late.

"Here is the map with the markings I drew myself." She said to me, either oblivious to what had occurred or genuinely not believing that I had seen what was on her screen. I looked at what she had on her phone screen and saw a picture of a forest near us that had some randomly crossed X's placed in a few spots, a few miles away from each other. It was probably a trap then.

I decided to keep it quiet until we arrived. She wouldn't do anything when we were all in the car, but because it was such an enclosed space, we wouldn't have the space to engage in a proper fight.

Fifteen minutes is all it took before we arrived at the first of the designated locations that she had marked on the map. We stepped out the car, Isabella first, with the rest of us lagging behind. Once we had got far enough away from the car so that she wouldn't be able to escape, I spoke up.

"When were you going to tell us?" I said, calmly.

"Huh? Who are you talking to?" Adam asked.

"About what Katie?" Lucy asked me, clearly worried that something was wrong, which it was.

"Are you going to answer?" I asked, leaving everyone's questions in the air. "I saw your calls; I know that it was you."

Everyone in the group looked at me as if I had grown a second head. As if I was crazy.

That was all interrupted by a low, slow laugh from in front. From Isabella, or whoever she actually was.

"So, you figured it out from my phone. I should've been more careful." She put her hands on her hips and shook her head, letting out another small chuckle.

The others head's whipped around, staring at Isabella hard.

"Isabella, what are you talking about?" Lucy asked her, a slight tremble in her voice. "You're joking around right?"

"Joking?" A violent laugh escaped her mouth. "You're a funny one, dear little sister."

As Lucy froze the others jumped into questioning.

"What do you mean Katie?" Drew asked. She trusted me but she would obviously want something that could clarify everything.

"I heard someone on the phone last night talking to someone at Kykl and promising how they were going to do great on their mission." I paused, staring right at Isabella's face. "The calls logs are at exactly the same time and end at the exact time I heard the talking."

"Maybe you misheard..." Adam offered thinly. Even after his friends confession he was understandably still trying to find a logical and fair reason to explain it. His care for his friends was one of his biggest qualities.

I shot him a look and he nodded at me. His attempt to explain the situation wasn't going to work in this circumstance.

"Let's go." I said descending on Isabella.

Like I had observed before, her fighting capabilities were much greater than what she had shown in all the other instances as she was matching me while having no weapons. This was something that I hadn't experienced before but I wasn't about to let this ruffle me. Drew was the next to jump in alongside me which gave an instant advantage, and realising that, Isabella started to run away, weaving through the open expanse of trees and foliage. Weaving through the brushes, I followed closely behind her, trying to catch up before she lost me. After only a few seconds I had nearly caught up to her, but she suddenly fell. What she hadn't noticed while trying to first fight me off with no weapons, and then both me and Drew, was that Vanessa had been setting up behind her in case of any escape attempt, which bore fruit straight away. I instantly pounced on her and although she struggled, she couldn't break free, which made Drew's job of tying her up, so she was immobile, even easier.

"Now," I started. "Who are you really?"

"Not Isabella." She said with a snort. "Although I don't know where that bitch is anymore."

"Why did you replace her? How do you look exactly like her?" Adam asked frantically.

"You're already too late so I guess I can tell you." She said, a frozen smile etched into her face. "We are going to change the world. You won't be able to stop us no matter how hard you try."

She let out a laugh that rattled everyone. I could see that the group who knew Isabella beforehand were struggling the most with this sudden change of events. Unlike us, they had known Isabella for a long time before we saved her from the Academy. I had suspected that something was off with her but this far surpassed my expectations. If the violated feeling and hurt that was bulging from my being from the betrayal of someone that I hadn't known for a long time was anything to go by, then I couldn't imagine what Vanessa and Adam were going through. But the one I was most worried about was her sister, Lucy.

Since the reveal, Lucy had frozen behind us. Although I didn't have time to console her right now, I was worried about what she might do. All the progress that she had made so far might be reversed because of Isabella not actually being real. Lucy was always around 'Isabella' and spent basically all her time with her no matter what the situation was. I glanced back and saw her frozen face, which I wasn't able to read, I instantly knew that something had changed inside her. Even in the worst situations she wore her heart open and proudly, and this was the first time that I had seen her face become unreadable. But right now, I needed to deal with this person who pretended to be Isabella.

"How do you look exactly like her?" I harshly asked.

"That's the way we are going to change the world. It is the same thing that Kykl has always been working on. Their life work and the procedure that is going to change the world." She continued with a smirk. "The ability to change anyone into any other person that they choose!"

What?

What could they possibly want that kind of ability for, I thought, but then it dawned on me.

Think big. Kings, Queens, Presidents, Prime Ministers. Everyone that they didn't like could easily get replaced by one of their people using this kind of method. No one would be safe. Nowhere would be safe. If they succeeded in their mission and got what they wanted, the world as we knew it would be over.

"No one can tell the difference between us and the real people. It is the perfect way to make the world a better place. The perfect way to stop all the bad people in the future."

"You do know how many people you are hurting and killing right now, right?" Drew asked, staring directly at the pretender.

"Sometimes sacrifices have to be made for the greater good. Nothing can be done without sacrificing at least something and that ranges from time, to things we have to do. The more you want to change, the more you have to be willing to sacrifice for the greater good."

By the end of her explanation, I felt as if I had a deeper understanding of what Kykl stood for and their goal. Changing the world into their ideal society. The reason why they wanted to do that was still a mystery to me though. Even though I had their action committed I didn't have their motive and didn't know why they wanted to change the world so much. Well, whatever their reason, they had now turned into the ones that needed stopping, who weren't trustworthy with their use of the influence and power they had and needed to be taken down.

"You're too late now, we've gone too far in our plan," She grinned maniacally. "You can't stop us from making ou-"

BANG

All the birds in our area flew away as the gunshot rang out. A bullet sized hole was in the fake Isabella's head, stopping her mid-sentence and not allowing anything to ever come from her mouth ever again, except blood.

I turned to where the shot had come from, and living up to my expectations, Lucy stood with her sniper rifle pointed at the girl, with a murderous look on her face.

"No one will do that to me ever again." She murmured.

I was wrong. I thought that she had taken steps back with her confidence and trust, but I was wrong. One look at her trembling hands that had dropped her gun and teary eyes showed me that this was done on pure impulse and she didn't really think about the consequences. As I was the closest one to her, I walked straight up to her and wrapped my arms around her. I was not one that gave out hugs much anymore but doing this with Lucy at this moment felt like the only way in which I could help her.

Check her body, I mouthed to Drew, indicating the fake Isabella dead on the ground. She nodded and then started going through her pockets to see if there was anything useful.

Lucy hugged me back, letting out soft sobs every now and then, but the incessant trembling failed to stop even after several minutes.

"Let's go back to the car." I said, taking her hand and leading her back as she nodded yes.

She could use a sit down right about now. Dealing with so much would eventually catch up with her if we didn't talk about it. I thought I might have been able to do that later, but right now was the best time considering how raw the memory would be in her head, on top of her tendency to overthink instead of just acting on instincts, which were almost always correct anyway. This was the first time she had acted purely by impulse and it was done in anger. If you aren't trained for moments like these, they could easily break you and ruin your life.

Once I had put Lucy in the car, I left, calling Vanessa over to stay with her. I wanted to see what they had found on fake Isabella's body.

"Here look." Drew said to me, handing over her phone. The screen showed the notes app and in there was one called 'Homebase' which listed some coordinates that, once I checked where they lead to, was only a few miles away from us.

"We should leave now." I said, handing Drew the phone back. "We were already prepared for infiltrating Kykl so we might as well carry on with our first plan of action now that we know the main base of operations for them is still in the same place as when Mary worked there."

"Yeah, let's go." Adam said, standing back up and walking towards the car, Drew and I trailing a little bit behind.

"We're going to have to do something to help Lucy." I said quietly to Drew. "She can't stay in this state, otherwise she could be putting herself in a lot of danger."

"She did the right thing." She looked over at me. "We had already got all the information we needed out of the Isabella thing so we can try and tell her that she was right in her decision?"

Before she had even finished, I was shaking my head. That wasn't the way to do this. She had killed her first person and not only was it someone who looked like her sister and was pretending to be her, but it was also done in anger, which was not something you wanted to mix together. Apart from reassuring, which might only help a little bit, there wasn't much that we could actually do to help Lucy. It was her own feelings that were weighing down on her. Her own actions that she committed voluntarily. Unless she came to terms with it herself, there was nothing more than support that we, the people around her, could provide. Right now, we needed to focus on the mission and make sure that Lucy wasn't spacing out and getting distracted in the middle of an inevitable battle as it would be detrimental.

"We need to keep her mind off it. We don't have time to talk her through her guilt and make her understand that it wasn't her fault either so we should just ignore what happened, for now, and focus on the mission." I said, just as we reached the car.

"Come on guys! We don't have all day!" Adam said, his whole body sticking out the driver's side of the car.

I smiled at the childish antics. Leave it to Adam to be the one motivating everyone and helping to lighten the mood. At first, I had assumed that he was just a person who relished being funny and made jokes just to get laughs, but after knowing him for as long as I had now, I now understood that wasn't the case at all. Intentionally making fun of himself and putting himself into funny situations, making jokes and trying to make people laugh, wasn't done for egotistical purposes. It was done to help out his friends. I could already see that his actions had made Lucy brighten up a bit and it made me appreciate him having another thing that I wasn't particularly good at; actually being funny when trying.

"Yes, yes we're coming." I said to him, rolling my eyes with a smile before getting in alongside him in the front.

I was glad that Kykl hadn't had as much time as they needed to grow because I was still able to use things like google maps without much of a fuss. If they got a satellite into space then their power and influence would instantly be raised exponentially and that was something I could not allow to happen.

"It is around here?" Adam questioned, as we exited the smallish town into a heavily wooded area.

"Yeah, it is around there." I said, pointing off into the tree line and signalling Adam to stop. "From now, we should continue on foot."

"Got it!" Adam said, pulling over in the tree line so that if someone walked past, they wouldn't be able to see the car.

"Where did you say the base was?" Vanessa asked me.

"It should be a few hundred meters that way," I pointed to where the tree line was most dense. "That is where Mary said and where the coordinates both lead to."

"Let's go over there then," Drew said, letting me take the lead.

As we walked along, the forest only got denser and denser. The few hundred meters that we walked felt more like a few miles because of the hindrance the thicket of foliage was causing. The vines slowed down our steps and made running impossible. The tall grass made stepping forward a chore and because of the abundance of useless forest in front of us, it made visibility ahead impossible.

"Stay close," I said to the rest who were behind me as the density increased yet again. "Grab my hand."

This forest seemed to be getting more and more clogged. If I didn't already have a good idea of where exactly it was that I was trying to navigate towards I would have already been lost. The more I thought about it, the more the idea didn't seem as crazy.

Because of how insanely dense and impenetrable this forest was, I was tempted to say that this wasn't a normally growing forest. It was most likely something that they had planted around their facility to make sure that no normal person was able to get in. If this was correct, it would also account for the fact that there were no traps. Having something like this would stop most people, even those with a good sense of direction, from getting through, but killing or injuring someone with traps would only bring more attention to themselves and that was definitely something that they did not want to deal with at all.

Just when I was questioning if we were still going in the right direction, we broke through the dense thicket into a long opening with a small abandoned looking building right in front of us.

"Finally..." Adam said, reflecting all our thoughts.

It was a nice feeling, finally being able to breathe properly. The stuffy nature behind us was suffocating and not something you would want to stay in for a prolonged period of time.

"Is this it though?" Vanessa asked, looking up at the small building, unimpressed with the unimposing, crumbling house that limped before us.

"Well these are the exact coordinates to it so it has to be here." I said, checking again to make sure I wasn't making any sort of beginner's mistake.

"Well, Ms. Bloom, you are correct and have impressed me quite a bit." A voice from inside the house suddenly spoke out, startling all of us and causing everyone to quickly turn to see who was there.

In the doorway to the dilapidated house stood a frail-looking, elderly man with thinning grey hair on top of his head and a full grey beard on his chin. He looked at us coldly, juxtaposing his warm and welcoming smile.

"Who are you?" I said, getting ready to fight him.

"I wouldn't do that if I were you," He said, and with a click of his fingers, I understood why. We had been surrounded. While we were too busy fussing over if this was the right place and just getting used to the normal non-claustrophobic air they had snuck up on all sides. All we had left was behind us to run. As quickly as the thoughts came, they disappeared into thin air. Everyone that was surrounding us had guns trained on our being. There was no way we could run or fight anymore. I felt my heart rate start to increase, which hadn't happened in a long time. I deepened my breathing to calm it down and only then did I realise why I was feeling like this.

I was scared. For the first time since my very first mission I felt a sense of helplessness. There was nothing I could do except to stand here and wait for them to kill us. I wouldn't be able to protect my family and friends. They would be able to do whatever they wanted to everyone I cared about and because I wasn't ready or prepared, I didn't have the reaction that I needed to avoid this predicament. All I could worry about right now was who the person in front of me was and what he was doing here.

"I have been watching you for a while Katie," He said, slowly moving closer to us. "Do you really think that I would come with people that you would beat so easily?"

At first, I had thought that he was some sacrificial pawn and from his frail body I had assumed myself to be right, but right now, I knew that I had never been more wrong. Something about him was different from everyone else that I had encountered. He had a much stronger aura and it seemed like he was used to controlling people like this. The air of authority surrounding him was something different. There was something about it which screamed 'Leader!' and it was only then that I finally put all the pieces together, and it seemed that this man knew it too.

"So, you finally figured it out then Kaite?" He asked with a sigh. "I expected you to be able to get it quicker from all I've heard about you so far, but I guess everyone was exaggerating when they said you were some prodigal genius."

"What did you figure out, I'm lost?" Vanessa whispered in my ear.

"Ah...Vanessa is it?" The old man said. "You see, I've been following all your group's movements since you formed together, and with renewed interest when I learned of Kaite and Drew's addition. You've been messing with my organisation too much now. I understand that you were just doing it to survive, but that doesn't make it right now does it?"

Vanessa was left speechless. She hadn't expected that he had been following her when she had only learned that his organisation wasn't just a myth very recently. Her face showed it clearly when the sentence finally sunk in that he was the leader of the whole of Kykl.

"Take them away." he said to some more guards, who came running out of the run-down house and started dragging us towards the broken-down structure.

I had wondered why they were dragging us into this small building until they opened a hatch inside and took us down the stairs to the bottom. It was like a whole new world down there.

Postmodern technology was strewn about everywhere, although there only appeared to be a couple of guards around. This made me feel even worse. They had been preparing for our arrival and knew exactly when we were coming, allowing them to be able to perfectly get into the best possible position to take us down. Just as I was thinking about trying to escape, the guards from upstairs started flooding down back into the underground bunker-like structure. I had almost made a costly mistake all because I wanted to make up for my earlier error in judging the situation.

"Come on, get in!" One of the guards said as they started to separate us into different lone cells far away from each other.

Lucy was, other than me, the last person in our group to get shoved in a cell and I saw the worry on her face and mouthed, it is going to be fine, with a little smile. While I was saying that for Lucy's sake, it was also to help myself. I had lost faith in my own abilities because of how many costly mistakes I had made that had eventually led us into this situation. That wasn't the part that I could fix. All I could do now was try and make the best of this bad situation and try and salvage us some leeway.

"Alright, come on out now." One of the guards said, once a few hours had passed, opening the door and waiting with his partner for me to get out of the cell.

Luckily for them, they had come with one person who had a gun, alongside one who didn't. If either was alone, I would've easily been able to take one out, but with two, it wasn't possible for me right now.

When we exited, I realised that none of my friends had come out and that it was only me.

"Hey, where are my friends?" I asked one of the guards who was leading me.

"Don't know don't care. Keep walking." The guard replied, harshly nudging me forwards with the front end of his gun.

The barren enclosed walls reminded me of the place where everything had started. It reminded me of all the time I spent locked inside the Academy walls, under the whim of Ana. The feeling I got from this place was also very similar. The disassociated coldness that was entrapping to anyone unlucky enough to experience. Adrenaline having run out, I was actually able to calmly take in everything that this place had to offer, but that also brought back all those horrible memories before I had closed my heart to strangers. That time when I was weak. Suddenly, it became harder to breathe and I slowed down again.

"Didn't I tell you to keep walking?" One guard behind me said, interrupting the oncoming panic and reminding me that I wasn't in that place anymore, and with my experience, I had the chance of escaping, which was much higher than it ever had been while stuck inside the Academy.

By the time I arrived at the leader of Kykl's room I had fully calmed myself down and was no longer feeling the same panicky feeling that had plagued my mind since I came out of the prison cell. The guard with the gun suddenly froze as the old grey-haired man came into view and he started to tremble.

"You know what to do." The old man said, glancing over at disgust at the man standing behind me.

The other guard handed him a knife and he walked out the room. In the distance not long after, I could hear a gurgle that I knew all too well. The gurgle that coincided with someone getting killed by having their throat slit.

"I've always hated guns..." The man grumbled under his breath, clearly in his own world, before realising that I was around too. "Ahh, Katie! It is lovely to see you again. I forgot to introduce myself before but my name is Xavier."

His words seemed sincere, but his expression was all I needed to see to know that he didn't hold me in a regard higher than a violent, wild animal.

"I brought you in here to try and get you to understand why I am doing what I am doing." He said, fingers steepled. "You have been one of the most successful candidates from the Academy that I had Ana Rodriguez run, who was one of my best strategists, and you surpassed even her. I am truly impressed by you and the innate talent that you have shown in both decision making in tough situations and also fighting ability after only training for a few months. You're a prodigy, simple as, and I want you on my side, so let me tell you why I am doing this."

Although there was no way in hell that I was going to join him at Kykl, I reasoned that getting angry or making him annoyed wouldn't help in this situation so I readily agreed to hear his plan, hoping to find out why he was doing this in the first   place.

"I was married when I was younger. I had just made my first few million and was on top of the world. That was until my wife was murdered for no reason." He said, closing his eyes as if to remember her face. "I tried to get the police to do an investigation but they didn't care at all. They passed me off as a rich spoilt kid and ignored everything I had to say, and that was when I came across Kykl. They were a company looking to change the world for the better and actually doing what they set out to do, which was exactly what I was looking for. I needed someone to agree with my vision and help me carry it out, which is why I bought Kykl with the help of some of my rich friends. Things were fine until they deviated from the goal and became part of the problem. I eventually, using resources from Kykl, found the people who killed my wife and hired someone to have them killed. Once I had killed them I knew that I was on the right track and doing the right thing, but I didn't have the money or resources to get everything I needed so I sent some employees to some extremely rich folk's houses and caught them doing crimes so horrible that even money couldn't make them go away."

"Like what...?" I asked.

"Anything from simple crimes like rape and murder to things like joining together with foreign governments and making plots to eradicate percentages of populations. After I got that material, I was set, as I had all their resources and money at my disposal and they couldn't go against me. I then had my best idea yet. Blackmail all the important leaders and get them to give me their thorough support and make sure that no one would be able to stop me making the world the best it can possibly be by taking things into my own hands and away from the incompetent officials who had been running the government for so long before I came along without getting anything of note done for a significant amount of time," He said, taking a second break to drink water. "I then started to rid the world of everyone doing anything that could get someone killed that didn't benefit the greater good."

Why do you get to decide what the greater good is? I thought, rolling my eyes.

"And that was when I realised that I needed more manpower." He indicated me. "The Academy was something that I created and managed for a while to provide me with the fully trained soldiers I needed, who were not only versatile but would also follow orders without having a purpose, which would eventually lead to them hearing about my plan and joining me fully, like Dr. Rodriguez or my latest assistant, the clone of Isabella, who both knew what I was doing but still fully supported me anyway."

"How can you be the only one deciding right from wrong?" I asked him, biting the bullet. "What about other people's opinions on what differs from right and wrong?"

He let out a small laugh before answering. "Look at where others butting into decisions got us. Look at the world around you and tell me that it isn't broken and doesn't need fixing."

"Of course, it does need fixing, but having one person at the helm will only breed more destruction."

"Okay," He said, letting out a sigh. "I see that you are not going to be joining me. I would've loved it but I cannot do anything about it right now." He stood up. "Get another guard from outside to take her back to her cell."

"Yes sir," The guard beside me said, leading me out of the room before handing me over to a smaller, more feminine guard who, from the moment she took control, was much gentler compared to the last guards.

"This isn't the way back to my cell!" I exclaimed, baffled as to where this person was taking me.

"I know Katie, I need your help," She took off her hat and stepped into the light, revealing Isabella!

This time I was sure that this wasn't a clone or anything like that. This time I was sure that she was the real thing.

"Isabella?" I asked. Although sure in my heart, my brain was still cautious.

"Yes, it is me," She said with a small smile.

"Wait, how do you know about me anyway?" I asked, suddenly realising that I hadn't interacted with her at all.

"I spoke to Lucy," She said. "And she mentioned how much you've helped her and the rest of the group. Thank you for looking after my sister and her friends."

Her sincerity wasn't something I doubted, seeing how much raw, crude emotion was filled in her voice and reflected in her eyes. She was genuinely happy, and unlike the last 'Isabella', seemed less jaded and more human. Less robotic and more natural. It was night and day compared to the image of 'Isabella' that I had gained from the clone.

"Right now, I need to go and see Xavier," I said to Isabella, nodding my head to indicate my acknowledgment of her thanks. "Do you know where my weapons are?"

"Yes, they are here, and, "She handed me my daggers, "the others said that we are moving to plan B now."

My heart jolted. I thought that there was no hope of all of us getting out of here alive, but the fact that they were able to get plan B underway showed that there was still a chance we could get out of here without suffering any casualties.

"I'll get going now." I said, "Be safe."

"You too."

There was nothing of any significance that blocked me from getting to Xavier's room. Although I came across a few guards, they all had no guns, courtesy of Xavier's hate for them, which was a real help in dealing with the multiple guards on route to Xavier's room.

As I got to his door, I saw the guards just changing and took advantage of this opportunity. I waited until they had just entered the room, not giving any time to set up and get comfortable and then burst into the room.

"Ah, Katie!" Xavier said with a light smile and waving off the guards who came to try and stop me from getting closer. "Have you changed your mind?"

"Hell no!" I grimaced at the mere thought of joining and aligning myself with him.

"Well, I didn't really expect anything else from you anyway."

"How many people are you killing who are just like your wife, to attain your goal?" I said firmly, trying to get him to see how wrong he was.

"I am only doing what is necessary to make sure that nothing like what happened to my wife can ever happen to an innocent victim ever again. What I am doing is the right thing to do as it makes the innocent people safer."

"What about all the girls at the Academy and their parents?"

"Change doesn't happen without sacrifice." He said, as if it was the most normal thing in the world. "These people are sacrificing for the greater good. They should be grateful that I am giving them a chance to contribute to the world so much."

His logic was so flawed and I honestly thought that he was trying to justify it to himself rather than explain it to me. But the grief he was experiencing wasn't something that I had control over and was something that only he could get past once he acknowledged it himself, which didn't look like it would happen any time soon.

"Well, as enlightening as this conversation has been, I've had enough of it." He went back to reading the documents on his desk. "Guards, take her back to her cell."

The guards moved away from the wall, but instead of coming towards me, they both went towards Xavier, each holding him by an arm.

"Ah! Hey, what are you doing?!" He angrily said, starting to lose his composure. "Didn't I tell you to take Kaite back to her cell?"

"Yeah, but who wants to listen to you?" One of the people holding his arms said.

They each dropped their hats to the ground revealing themselves and it was then that Xavier understood what went had happened.

"You! Katie, you planned this all along!" He spat, trying to wrench free but not being able to gain any leverage. "Guards! Guards!"

"You should've known that it would come to this eventually, right?" I said. "If all you do to get people to work for you is threaten and blackmail them, they are eventually going to snap, having had enough, and because you've done it with nearly everyone, it was a piece of cake to convince them to switch sides. Being scary doesn't work if you haven't been able to back it up for a long time because you lost all your trusted subordinates."

"Impossible!" He shouted, "They wouldn't betray me like this!"

His shouting was getting louder and louder and more annoying by the second so I got the left guard, Drew, to tape his mouth shut while Vanessa, the guard on the right, held him back, with my help.

"What should we do to him then?" Vanessa asked me.

"We should take him out so that nothing can ever happen to anyone by his hand again," Drew said, her fists clenched. She was probably thinking about her mother and how much she suffered in her relationship with her and had to rebuild it from scratch again because of this despicable man.

I thought long and hard about it, consulting Drew and Vanessa, but we couldn't come up with anything that wasn't just killing him outright.

I looked at Xavier deeply and saw the hatred he had for us at that moment, but what I saw behind that was a normal man. A man who just wanted his family and everyone he loved to be cared for, someone that society had just thrown away. And that was when it hit me like a speeding truck.

I knew what to do with Xavier now.

"We aren't going to kill him." I finally said.

"We can't just let him go though!" Vanessa blurted. Confused by my decision.

"We aren't going to let him go," I explained. "We are going to get everything here that proves all the crimes that he has committed and then hand him over to the police."

"I can just get my soldiers to testify for me or pay off the judges." He smirked. "You can't keep me locked up."

"Do you really think that anyone was actually following you because they believed in the mission?" Harshly explaining, I continued. "No one will save you from what you've done here."

"Look at all the people I have under me that have all that money and influence! That is all mine to use whenever I want!" Xavier said whilst sweat started to pour down his face at an alarming rate.

"Right now, everything that you have, all the blackmail material, is being deleted," I said, watching his nonreaction. "We've found where you store all the backups. You really need to keep a watch on what your subordinates carry." I pulled out a piece of paper with the coordinates of four different places and waved it in front of him.

"Also, we know that you haven't put any clones into any positions of power yet, so we messaged your lab to destroy all the research," Drew said.

"Y-you should be listening to me! I am invincible and everyone will help me because if they don't, I will ruin them!" He was breathing hard, going past his breaking point.

This was when I realised that Xavier wasn't a mastermind or anything of the sort. He just had good connections because of his diligent work blackmailing successful people. He on his own could do nothing as he was a coward at heart. The only people he dealt with in person were ones he viewed as lower than him and because of that, he was now unable to do anything in the face of adversity, not even something as simple as keeping a calm and collected head. He portrayed himself as an infallible master of the dark, but the truth was, he hid behind someone else the second his life was in danger. He didn't inspire confidence or belief in any of his subordinates and they weren't going to follow him anymore.

He then pulled out a small clear button and pressed it. "You better apologise to me now because if you don't, I'll tell the guards to kill you when they come."

His arrogance really knew no bounds and it was fun to see the expression on his face when his soldiers finally came into the room but didn't move from the spot.

"I've deleted everything you have on all of these guys already and I have told them that there is no way that anyone will be able to access any information again." I shook my head. "If you want people to follow you, you need all of them to believe in the project that you are working on, otherwise it ends up like this."

"You...!" He trailed off after looking around and seeing everyone staring at him with such disdain.

His arrogance was his downfall. Once upon a time, he may have been a lot more cautious and stored his information without writing things down, but nowadays, because he had never been caught and had only succeeded, he got arrogant and cocky and that led to his downfall. You could get cocky if you had people to back you up after the fact but, unlike me with my friends, he had no one to slap him back down when he got too full of himself, which was detrimental to his victory.

"Can you guys gather up everything you think is evidence and bring it out front?" I asked the soldier who replied by carrying out the task without any complaints.

Xavier looked broken seeing everyone that was beside him now walking away with no regard for him. In fact, most were actively ignoring him.

Isabella then entered the room and walked to me.

"I found the guy who was investigating this place. He lives a few miles away from here and from what I can find, he hasn't had any leads yet. Xavier even leaked the logo to the guy because he was so confident that he wouldn't find it."

"Why don't we go and give this guy a little present then, yeah?" I said, indicating Xavier and all the evidence that was being moved out of this room.

"I'm so tired..." Adam said.

"You haven't even been doing anything. It was all Isabella, Drew, and me," I exclaimed.

"I know, but watching you guys do all that work has made me so tired." Adam lazed.

"Well, I mean we are home now," Lucy said. "It is going to be so nice living so close to friends from now on."

"And now we have money!" Adam said, suddenly energetic. "We're rich!"

"I have money, you're just a freeloader," Isabella said. "Living off of me."

"Alright, alright kids, we've arrived." I said as I drove back into my hometown.

I had always known how to drive but I wasn't amazing at it so in the situations where we had to move fast, I wasn't the best choice, but it didn't mean I was incapable of driving, and because of the money we had received I had decided to get a car for myself.

I didn't have many expectations that I would be back here after going on the dangerous mission of taking down Kykl and the ideas were firmly flushed down the drain once I was captured by Xavier, but in the end, everything had turned out okay. In fact, it had turned out so much better than I had thought it would in the end.

Once we had given Xavier and all the evidence over to the black ops agent, we then went through a month-long process where Xavier was eventually convicted because of all the people who came out against him once they realised that their livelihoods were stable and nothing was going to come along and ruin their lives. The weight and power of all these people got Xavier put in jail for the rest of his life in a maximum-security prison. He was already old, but with the number of things he did, he wasn't getting out for the rest of his life due to the five hundred and thirty two consecutive life sentences he was given, which I later found out was the longest in the UK by a long margin. But I wasn't that surprised considering how many people he had killed and how many other major crimes he had committed. A few others who had committed crimes because of being blackmailed were arrested alongside him and were given a few years, but most of the people were acquitted. All the people that he had kidnapped were able to claim compensation as there was a list that had been kept. So, Isabella, Drew, and I all got a lot of money from the divided assets that used to belong to Xavier and we would never have to worry about money anymore.

"We are here." I said, pulling into the driveway.

Alongside my car, was a ruby red Honda S2000. Jessica!

I hadn't seen her in such a long time. She and Jill weren't there the last time I came back here, and it had already been a few long, gruelling months since our last encounter.

As I was thinking this, the door burst open and all I saw was a flash before a human jumped onto me.

"Katie!" Jessica screeched, smiling wide whilst hugging my tight. "I'm so glad you're back"

I felt my heart swell looking at her. Since I had last seen her, she had matured a lot physically, but it was nice to know that she was still the same girl who had been my friend since childhood. This was a warmth I hadn't felt before, as the last time I was here, I was still struggling with everything that had been going on. I wasn't ready to have my friends back, but now I was, and taking full advantage of it was what I wanted to do, so I hugged her back.

"Katie, you're back!" Another voice said as they walked out the door.

Walking towards me was Jill, smiling wide as she got closer. While Jessica was glued to one side of me, Jill hugged me on the other. When trying to take down, first the Academy and then Kykl, I was more focused on trying to complete the mission and survive than thinking about all the friends I had back home. I was only now realising how much I had missed their company, because even with all my other friends I had made along the way, these people were with me before I was taken and had stuck with me after that. They were different from my other friends, but it didn't mean that I appreciated either side any less. From two completely different times in my life, me being such a different person when I made all these friends, it finally felt like my two lives were merging together with this gathering.

"I missed you guys too," I said back to them, squeezing them tightly before letting go as the last person who I had been waiting for exited the house.

My mother. Although it hadn't been long since I left her and I had already seen her recently, leaving her while she was feeling so distressed about what I was doing was something I could've regretted for the rest of my life if things had gone differently. Her face, which was now devoid of all worry and was now just filled with love, looked more youthful, as now, the stress that was on her had been washed away.

"You came back." She said as she came in for a hug.

I was getting hugged more in this short minute-long window than I had in the past few months - not that I was complaining at all. In fact, I was really enjoying all this close physical affection that I was getting to experience again, but especially from my mum.

While I was close to Drew and she did help me out with physical comfort, as I did with her, it didn't reduce how much a mother's hug can make you instantly feel better and more alive. All my stresses and worry had been wiped away in an instant.

In the back of my mind, I had still been thinking about the possibility of Xavier sending one of his goons to try and hurt my family behind my back, but he never thought that far ahead, or maybe he did and that person just defected and didn't want to carry out those orders. No one knew what the real case was here, and frankly, I didn't care. My family were safe and sound, my friends happy and succeeding more in life than they had ever been in the past and there wasn't another organisation that was trying to kill us, which was always a positive.

The future was still an unknown, but right now, I didn't need to worry about that. I was going to enjoy this time with everyone as much as possible and appreciate it for the rest of my life.

EPILOGUE

Three years later.

"Your cooking is so good mum," I said, smiling at my mother. "I don't think I will ever get tired of it."

"Oh, you..." She said, smiling at me in a teasing way. "You don't have to continue to flatter me."

She said that but I could see that her confidence and ego were driven higher by my words. Oh well, she had been taking care of me to the best of her ability for the past few years, so I wasn't going to complain or contradict her.

I think that she still felt guilty about 'letting me get taken' (which were her exact words) and no amount of convincing on my part could stop her feeling that way. She would say that she understood and was fine but later on, I would find she was going out of her way to help me out (even more so than she usually would) and also worrying about me and panicking if I went off without telling her. It had been a bit of a hassle dealing with her, but it was something that I had to deal with and I would do anything so mum didn't have to go through an experience like that ever again.

"Drew, take some of these," Mary said, putting some food on Drew's plate.

Although Drew had the money to buy her own house and either live there with Mary, her mother, or get another house so that she could live apart from her mother, she hadn't even thought of doing that. When I suggested that, she just plainly said no, not even thinking about it for a second before rejecting my proposal and since then, she had been living here with her mother.

At first, she had been cold to her mother, but after a few months she had started to warm to her, and now...well...

"Yes, mum!" Drew said, smiling widely as she accepted the food, staring at her mother lovingly.

...She had turned into that...

I wasn't complaining. It was a pleasant change and it was nice to see her so happy, as if she hasn't experienced life in the Academy, but it took a lot of getting used to over the past few years.

Although not as much as Drew, I had changed too. I had started to face my struggles head-on and it really had helped me, especially with the panic attacks I used to have every few months. At the time, I didn't recognise most of them as such, but looking back to how I felt and comparing them to what a panic attack actually felt like, it wasn't even a question as to whether I had or not. I knew I had.

I also finally got a job. Throughout the years I hadn't been thinking of getting a job because of all the money I had saved up, but after a while, I realised that I wasn't happy just sitting around all day or doing my own thing. I wanted a challenge in my life and that was when I tried applying for jobs. Over the first few months, a few accepted my applications, but they were mundane jobs like working in a shop chain and I always ended up quitting because of how boring it was. My past experiences had ruined what I would consider normal and satisfying. I was then approached by the black ops agent who we had given Xavier over to along with all the evidence. At the trial, he had approached me and said that he would love to speak to me at a later date. That date being a few months down the line.

What he had offered me was the ability to control my own black ops squad working in the same place he did. He got all the credit for bringing down the Kykl, but he knew what had really happened and put in a word with the higher-ups. We had brokered a deal that comprised of Drew, Isabella, Lucy, Vanessa, Adam, and me, forming the team that could go on missions whenever we felt like it. It felt like a dream job to me as I could use the only real-world skills that I had accumulated in my short stint of life so far.

At first, when I told mum, she was vehemently against it, not entertaining any sort of argument that I brought to the table to try and convince her to support my decision. It wasn't until the people in charge of the black ops team came and explained the risks and perks that she started to give some leeway. She still wasn't happy, but once she saw how safe it actually was she was more willing to let me do as I pleased, because she now was able to see how happy I was with this job compared to all the others. Through the years that I had this job, she eventually learned to accept it and was now content to see me off without any problems. She still worried, don't get me wrong, but she now treated it like any normal job that contained a little bit of danger, because with my skills and the skills of the people I worked with being so good, we didn't have too much to worry about on these missions.

The depth they went into when explaining what we needed to do to prepare for a mission wasn't new to any of us, but the safety precautions were something we didn't have the luxury of having before - Planning escape routes; Making sure that there was always a way to escape being trapped once spotted; Making sure that communication was available at all times, and also making sure that we had a way to fight off a multitude of enemies at the same time. Apart from the communication devices at the Academy, these weren't things that we consistently had access to use to ensure safety.

The first mission we went on as a squad proved why all that safety work was in place and showed how being prepared can easily save your life.

Drew, Vanessa, Isabella, and I had quickly and quietly fought off and taken down all the guards. We decided to go separate ways to make the mission go quicker because once the first few guards had been taken down, we foolishly looked down upon the others as if they were the same people with the same skill sets, which definitely wasn't the case. Once split up, we still maintained communication and made sure to check in but it was not long after that that Isabella had encountered a room packed full of guards. Without the precautions in place, she very likely would've been hurt or even killed by those people.

Luckily for her, she had one of the incapacitating bombs with her that allowed her to take down all those guards. It wasn't something that we usually used as it could also potentially take us out if we weren't prepared (gas mask) so having to use it like that was a shock.

Since that incident, we had been much more cautious and made sure to be one hundred percent sure on any call that could lead to danger because we were still risking our lives no matter how easily some of these missions got completed.

I felt my phone buzz in my pocket just as I had finished putting the dishes in the dishwasher.

"We have to go Drew," I said, showing her the text from the group.

"Okay," She replied, wiping her hands clean. "Just let me get ready. You go ahead."

"Okay, see you there." I said, pushing my chair back in. "Bye mum!"

I hugged her and then left the house, the chill being pleasant as I walked along.

I had been home for a long time but that didn't mean that I had got used to everything back here. Even now, I admired all the scenery.

Being Autumn, the red to yellow gradient blended into the bright, colourful sunset, adding to the majestic, magical feeling.

I hadn't had much time to myself to just relax and enjoy something over the last few years. Life had been moving too fast, but now that I had more time to explore and find hobbies that I enjoyed, I was going to take full advantage of it and let my desires take the driving seat.

Nostalgia rarely visited anymore, and I rarely thought about. While walking closer to my friends I caught a glimpse of red hair walking towards me. At first, I thought it could be Drew or her mum but that wasn't realistic at all.

It was only then that I realised it was a guy. Someone from my past life. Someone who I used to know.

Blake.

In the years I had been gone he had changed a lot. He was much better looking, more mature, compared to what he used to be, which wasn't surprising considering we were both kids when we first saw each other.

He was someone I hadn't thought about in years. Back then he was, and still is, the only guy I've ever liked.

What would my life have been like had I not been kidnapped?

I knew that we liked each other, but would we still be together?

What would our lives look like together? Would we be happy or not? In a healthy relationship or not?

These were all questions that I had thought about when I first got kidnapped, but since then I hadn't given it the time of day.

We then walked past each other, neither of us acknowledging the other. Maybe he didn't even recognise me, and I felt myself rejuvenate.

I didn't need to think of what if's because, in the end, they didn't matter. I was happy with my life now, and although the path to recovery was long, it was also exciting. Seeing someone from what felt like a past life had only reinforced those feelings. I didn't want to go back, and I wouldn't change any of what I had experienced. It made me the person I was today, and those experiences were helping me grow into the person that I would be tomorrow.

Maybe in the past I would've wished to have my previous life and the present live combined into one, but I was okay with leaving some things behind, including some of the people that I used to know and was friendly with, while others, Jessica and Jill, were as much support for me as I was to them.

In the end, Blake and I weren't meant to be, but he did help me grow in certain ways. He was the first step in the process of giving me the life that I loved and enjoyed today, even though he would never be a part of it.

In the distance I saw my friends, the new ones I had made, standing there, waiting for me. Drew had also just arrived because she had jogged. I felt content.

I didn't need everything that I used to had back. I didn't want it either.

I was happy with what I had now and the friends that have supported me through everything.

My friends. My family. They were what helped day by day and what made me realise that I was happy now.

"You all ready?" I asked.

"Yep!" Drew happily responded, which was echoed by the rest. "Let's go now!"

Looking around at their happy faces I could never imagine anything else. A smile came over me and I looked forward, ready for whatever the next adventure would hold.

The end

ACKNOWLEDGEMENTS

It has been a long, challenging and fun filled journey in which the first chapter of many has been completed. It has been a pleasure writing this book, and, after all this time, being able to see it in its final form is an unexplainable feeling.

To my family who supported my thorough everything. You inspire my every day. I'll never forget the helpful work that you all contributed towards in making this book the best it can be.

Printed in Great Britain
by Amazon